Chasing Me

SEX ON THE BEACH #2

Copyright © 2014 by Jennifer Probst

All rights reserved. No part of this book may be reproduced, transmitted, downloaded, distributed, stored in or introduced into any information storage and retrieval system, in any form of by any means, whether electronic or mechanical, without express permission of the author, except by a reviewer who may quote brief passages for review purposes, if done so constitutes a copyright violation.

This book is a work of fiction. Names, places, characters and events are fictitious in every regard. Any similarities to actual events and persons, living or dead, are purely coincidental. Any trademarks, service marks, product names, or named features are assumed to be the property of their respective owners and are used only for reference. There is no implied endorsement if any of these terms are used.

Manufactured in the United States of America

ISBN-13: 9781621252368

Chasing Me

SEX ON THE BEACH #2

JENNIFER PROBST

Dedication

"If you live to be a hundred, I want to live to be a hundred minus one day so I never have to live without you." ~ A. A. Milne

"Pains of love be sweeter far than all the other pleasures are." -- John Dryden

To all my readers who are chasing something wonderful. I hope you find it.

Prologue

IT WAS SUPPOSED TO BE A LOVE STORY.

Right?

Yeah, I know, I didn't believe in that shit. Lust? Hell, yeah. Love?

No fucking way.

Yet here I am, alone in my apartment, on my knees, staring at a closed door. 'Cause she left me. For good this time. And if she was smart, she'll never take me back, because all I do is end up hurting her and screwing up her life. She deserves better, and that's not me. Yet the idea of another guy putting his hands on her makes me want to roar like the animal I am and beat the life out of him. Quinn's always affected me that way.

I remember the first time I saw her.

A one-piece swimsuit covering her slamming body, eyes dark and mysterious as she met my gaze with that haughty look I'd get to know and adore. In that moment, I fell head over fucking heels and never looked back.

I knew she was out of my league, but I didn't care. Looking back, I wonder if I hadn't pursued her, would things have turned out differently? Is it Fate that determines our choices in life? God? Free will? Or just plain old innate selfishness?

I got her, of course. There hadn't been a girl I wasn't able to seduce. Problem was, she seduced me right back, body, mind, and fucking soul. She possessed me, tormented me, and showed me a world that was so bright and pure I was almost blinded.

Quinn made me feel alive again, reconnecting me with a part of myself I thought I'd buried years ago. She looked right into my sorry soul and loved me anyway. Didn't she know after such a drug I could never settle for less? Didn't she realize no matter how many times I screwed up, or broke her heart, or bent her to my will, I'd never be able to let her go?

If I hadn't known such intensity existed, would it have been better for both of us?

I don't pretend to have any of the answers. I never did. All I know is when she left me in Key West, I had to make a choice. The week we spent together in Key West was a sliver of a possible future, a future filled with more meaning than I'd ever had in my pathetic twenty-four years. I could change my life and go after her, into another dimension I had no experience with. I could leave my friends and my shit behind and start fresh, and become the man I wanted to be for her. A man she seemed to glimpse in my eyes, even though I still worried day after day if that man even existed.

Now, I know he never did.

But it's too late. I followed her to Chicago, enrolled in art school, and swore I'd be everything she wanted. For a while, it was as perfect as I imagined. Then, like I always do, I made a wrong choice and watched my future and the love of my life disappear in a cloud of smoke that choked my lungs and reminded me of my limitations.

Yeah, did you think this was a fucking love story?

Sorry to dissuade you, but you better go down to your local bookstore and pick some other shit up. Unless you're like me, and believe true love, the real kind, isn't nice and sweet and pure. No, it's dirty, and sinful, and messy. It's like ripping a chunk of flesh from your body and watching yourself bleed out in slow, helpless intervals until you thankfully pass out.

No. This isn't a love story. But it's the only story I got.

Let's hope the ending hasn't been written yet.

Chapter One
Quinn

"HEY, QUINN, THEY NEED YOU IN Room SEVEN!"

I nodded, my sensible loafers squeaking over the polished floor of the senior citizen home, passing the night nurse who was struggling with Mr. Pearson to swallow his meds while he screeched that they were trying to poison him and begged for someone to save him.

I hardened my heart, though I just wanted to throw Nurse Crotchet off him and give him the lollipop I carried in my pocket for those freak-outs that my patients seemed to have. But the last time I had challenged her, she threatened to tell the supervisor I was a problem, and I didn't need any issues when graduation loomed so near.

I took a right and swung into Mrs. Apple's room, trying not to wince at the shrieks echoing down the hallway. I'd been working at the center for a year now, and had gotten to know all the patients on a one-to-one basis. I took my job seriously, even though I was only paid minimum wage and considered a part-time basic caretaker, but if I did well, I might get a permanent position while I waited for a full-time opening at the New Beginnings Rehabilitation Clinic.

Usually I liked the center and found both the staff and residents pleasant. Most people think of senior centers as smelling of old people and disinfectant; white hospital gowns and patients shuffling down corridors with a mad look in their eyes. Unfortunately, there were too many state nursing homes, but this residence catered to the elderly who still had their functions and were able to make sense of where and who they were.

The cheerful yellow walls were set off with paintings and framed words of ancient wisdom, hopefully allowing the residents to think of the positive things in life rather than why their son or daughter hadn't visited them in too many weeks.

But I pushed all these muddled thoughts from my head and stopped at Mrs. Apple's bedside. "Quinn! There you are, sweetheart. I don't want to go to bed yet. I'd like to read in my chair please, but they're giving me a hard time."

I smiled and did my normal routine, plumping and smoothing out her pillows, and pretending to fix her blankets. "It sounds like a wonderful idea, Mrs. Apple, but remember you need some extra sleep tonight? You're having blood work super early in the morning, and they won't let you eat or drink. When you read, you always get thirsty."

The eighty-year-old scrunched up her face in deep thought. I kept up my busy motions, knowing she craved attention at night, when the demons came by to visit. "I forgot. Didn't I have my blood work yesterday?"

I tried not to grin, because she was damn sharp. "This is a different blood test. Oh, your nail polish is chipping off. How about I re-do them tomorrow? What color do you think you'd like?"

She lifted her hands, heavily veined with brown spots. But her nails were squared off with pretty pink polish that sparkled under the dim light. A soft smile curved her lips. "Something different. Maybe purple?"

I shook my head and made a tight crease in the sheets, bringing them up to her waist. "Well, my goodness, you are getting a bit wild on me. Do you want to give Mr. Foster a heart attack? He already can't keep his eyes off you."

She cackled out a giggle. "Stop playing with me, child. Everyone knows he's having a thing with Emma."

I raised my brow. "For real? How come no one told me?"

"You can't keep secrets."

I gasped. "I'm a great secret keeper!"

Mrs. Apple surrendered to the pillow and let out a sigh. "Everyone knows you break under duress. Your heart is too kind." Her lids slid closed, an effect of the mild sedative she'd just received. "Why aren't you with your young man? He must miss you."

I brushed the stray silver hair from her forehead. "He's waiting at home for me. Good night. Sleep tight."

"Good night, Quinn."

I made sure to tiptoe out and pull the door closed. Pushing past a tired sigh, I glanced at my watch. One more hour to go. After a full day of classes, and the night shift this week, I was ready to collapse. I hadn't spent any quality time with James in a few days, and I missed him. Funny, in the past months, he'd become my rock in a pit of shifting sand. I'd changed since returning last year from Key West, when our idyllic week spent in the sun, fiercely falling hard for each other, blew up when I found out he'd made a bet with his friends to get me into bed. When I got on that plane and left him behind, returning to my normal routine in Chicago, I'd gone through the motions with an empty ache in my gut.

And then he followed me to Chicago.

A shiver bumped down my spine. I'd never forget that moment I saw him strolling across campus, his midnight hair blowing in the wind, pale-blue eyes trained on me with a raw possession and claim that still got me hot. He'd come for me, to make a life in Chicago and see if we could make it together. To me, there'd been no choice but to forgive him and give him a chance. I mean, I loved him, heart and soul. The way he overtook my body with just a dominating glance, the way he tenderly stroked my hair from my face, or made me laugh. The way he held my wrists, and pushed between my thighs while he whispered how I belonged only to him. He'd taken away every choice, and given me only one. Him. Completely.

James Hunt was my everything.

On cue, my phone shook in my pocket. I slid it out, glanced at the screen, and hit the button. "Hey, I was just thinking of you."

His low chuckle rippled my nerve endings. "Was I naked?"

How was it possible I still blushed when he spoke dirty to me? "No. At least, not yet," I teased back.

"Too bad. 'Cause I was thinking of you. And you were definitely naked. You also had a bottle of chocolate syrup in your hand. Now, what do you suppose you were doing with that?"

"Wouldn't that be awfully sticky and hard to clean up afterward?"

His laugh vibrated through the phone. "Practical to the end, my Quinn. I'd make it worth the cleanup."

"Bet you would. How was class?"

His pause spoke volumes. My heart beat in my chest, but I tried to remind myself he needed to find his way, and all I could do was support him.

"Fine."

Lying by omission. I pushed harder. "Did you work on portraits today?"

This time, he let out an irritated breath. "You don't need to worry about me. I never expected this to be easy, or waltz into art school while my teacher declared me the best-kept secret and promised me fame and fortune."

"Damn, I did."

His laugh broke the tension. "Yeah, would've been nice. Still coming over? I made some pasta for you."

Exhaustion didn't matter to me as much as sleeping entwined with him, the sound of his heart beating against my ear. Our places were relatively close, and most nights we spent together, but my dad would freak if he thought we were living together. Besides, we both needed our own space for now. "Definitely."

"Good. I'll see you in an hour."

"James?"

"Yeah?"

"Love you."

His voice dropped. "Prove it when you get here."

The click sounded in my ear. I pushed my cell phone back into my pocket and headed toward the kitchen for cleanup duty. The minute I saw James's portraits, hidden in the attic of his mansion in Key West, I knew he had exceptional talent. The way he was able to capture the emotion on the strangers' faces made them no longer strangers. He'd refused to do anything with his art, hiding it from his friends and parents, until he showed up in Chicago, ready to try. Enrolling in the up-and-coming art school—Brush Institute of Art & Design—was key. Admission was tricky, and just the fact that he was in proved he had talent.

Unfortunately, he wasn't used to strict discipline with his classes, especially basics he'd already mastered. His teacher seemed to be on a crusade to tear him down in front of his other classmates, making the past few months difficult. I wished I could help in some way, but he was determined to take care of things himself. I think it had to do with his past responsibilities, or rather, lack of them. He'd been a college dropout, huge partyer, and frat-boy extraordinaire.

But I believed in him. Always did. Always would.

We were in this journey together, and the future was bright. I'd finally graduate from Chicago State, begin internship at the rehab, maybe work on my master's in social work, while James took the art world by storm. Sure, it wouldn't be easy. I'd learned in my life long ago that nothing was, but I also believed that hard work paid off. Paying my dues.

All in all, not such a bad deal.

I lifted my chin with determination and focused on getting through the next hour before getting some well-needed rest.

Chapter Two
James

I HUNG UP THE PHONE AND stared with disgust at my current drawing. The lines were bold enough, the light and shadow contrast decent, but something was missing. The element of emotion and intensity that usually transferred onto the board and gave the sketch life.

This was bullshit.

I grabbed the half-finished drawing and shoved it into the closet, slamming the door in a toddler tantrum that made me choke. I was tanking, and pissed off. When I got into Brush Institute, I thought it would be the first step into making my art into a career that would be productive one day. I mean, let's be honest, I'm a literal spoiled rich boy who lives off his parents' money. Funny, it used to bother me before, but not enough to change things. Now, with Quinn in my life, desperate to make an impression on her and her Dad, each obstacle before me seemed harder.

My admission test placed me at a high entry point, which meant I got to skip a lot of bullshit classes for beginners.

Guess my book studies and years of practice on my own had given me a good start. But when I tried to get into the more advanced classes, my current teacher from hell blocked me.

Ava Goodridge.

She was both talented and recognized in the art world for her fierce manner in watercolors and bold sketches of the male form. Not my usual cup of tea, but she was a force of creativity and energy I couldn't deny.

Unfortunately, she fucking hated my guts.

I grabbed a beer from the refrigerator and sat at the table brooding, waiting for Quinn. From the very first meeting, Ava had looked at my work with a cool disregard that burned in my gut. And instead of approving me for the painting and portrait classes I wanted to take, she denied me. Stuck me in an elementary drawing class, telling me I needed to relearn my mechanics.

For the past four months, I worked my ass off to impress her. Nothing did. Her suggestions and subtle insults to my work were well known in class. My peers looked at me with sympathy when she used me as an example of what I did wrong on all counts. Didn't matter how I responded, either. If I was quiet and took her shit, she dubbed me a disinterested learner. If I defended my position or tried to explain, she cut me off with a withering glance and told me I was there to get better, not defend crap.

She tied me up in knots until I questioned everything about what I was doing. But I needed to hang tight, get through the rest of the semester, and show her what I had. I also needed to prove to Quinn that I could take the shit with dignity. I was done with running or looking for the easy way out. God knew, Quinn showed me with her own sense of responsibility and work ethic that she needed a man to match her. Someone worthy of her love. Not a rich kid who depended on his parents' millions and spent his life jet-setting with a bunch of assholes, partying nonstop. No, not anymore.

I was gonna make sure I didn't fail.

The door opened. I was used to the slight shock I always got when I looked at her. Something about her gorgeous dark eyes, so open and honest, with the spill of her chocolate-brown hair and amazing body. Her skin was soft and warm and responsive to anything I wanted to do with her or to her. Our sexual chemistry was a force I'd never experienced before. Even standing in a room, it was like a buzz of electricity always hummed between us. Yeah, I sound whipped, right? Funny, I didn't give a crap anymore. She was my drug of choice, and I needed a steady hit, or I'd go bat-shit crazy.

She pulled off her jacket and hat, tossing it on my worn couch I'd gotten used, and gave me that smile that kicked my heart into gear and made my dick so hard it could cut stone. "I'm hungry," she announced.

I gave her a slow grin, stalking her until she pressed back against the door, those dark eyes going all intense and foggy. God, I loved how just my look got her all hot. With Quinn, a few touches and she was so wet for me, her needy groans vibrating in my ear, making me feel like a fucking god.

"So am I." I reached her, running my fingers through her silky hair and beginning to unbutton her pink flannel shirt. The little catch of breath told me she didn't mind waiting for dinner, and she enjoyed our little games just as much as me. Raw hunger ripped at me. I swallowed the crazy need to tear off her clothes and fling her to the ground, shoving myself deep into her wet heat. Instead, I fought back the intensity and dragged in a breath. Quinn deserved gentleness and worship. Not being treated like an animal. I needed to control my caveman reactions, even if it almost killed me.

I parted the material and gazed at her simple white bra. She liked to surprise me. Sometimes she'd wear the sexiest, laciest underwear and tell me about it when we were in a public place, knowing it made me nuts. Other times, she played the innocent, with white bra and cotton panties.

Funny, I think the virginal stuff revs me up even more.

I managed to calmly flick the clasp of her bra open. Her red nipples were already tight and hard, begging for my tongue, and she arched up like a pretty present just for me. I palmed the gorgeous globes of flesh while she quickly unfastened my jeans with an expert ease that always impressed me. Quinn may have looked innocent and sweet, but she was the hottest, most responsive woman I'd ever been with, her arousal so intense sometimes my cock wept for the feel of her tight, slick folds clasping me in a vise. She also loved dirty talk, one of my favorite things in bed.

"How bad do you want it?" I asked, tonguing her nipples and sucking hard on the tips. She paused in the act of ripping my pants off, her fingers curling into the rough denim as she gasped, wiggling to get closer.

"Bad," she moaned. "No teasing."

I bit down just enough to wrack a shudder from her body. Already, I felt like I was ready to come, and I wasn't even out of my jeans. She made me insane with the drive to mark her, possess, claim. Thank God she wore stretchy yoga-type pants, so I was able to yank them down with one hard tug. She stepped out of them, and sure enough, there were the cotton panties covering her sweet pussy. I smelled her arousal, and when my hand palmed her over the fabric, they were already damp.

I wanted to pull my cock out and plunge inside her tight heat with one deep thrust. Instead, I lifted my head from her tits, and studied her gorgeous face. Eyes closed, lips parted as pants of breath escaped, she was all mine and crazy for me. She deserved to be with a man who was controlled, not one who'd go right to a rough, intense fuck against the door.

"Come with me," I said roughly, tugging at her hand.

Those eyes widened in foggy confusion. "No, here. Right now."

I growled low in my throat, barely hanging on. "You should have a bed."

I tried to step away, but she grabbed me hard, grinding her hips against my erection until I gritted my teeth, knowing

I'd never make it to the bedroom now. I shoved down my underwear, pushed her back, and lifted her high. She shook with excitement, but I made sure I was back in control.

"Bossy girls get punished," I said in her ear. My fingers swiped her wet slit and she gave a low moan, her hips lifting for more. I pushed two fingers slow and deep, thumbing her clit with teasing brushes, not allowing her to get off until I'd driven her out of her mind. "Tell me you're mine."

"I'm yours. James, please." She twisted in my grasp, and I took her mouth in a long, deep kiss, my tongue thrusting in the same tempo as my fingers. Her nails dug into my shoulders, begging for more, but I refused, trying to wring out every sweet, hot moment before she came. Not able to wait another second, I replaced my finger with my cock, bareback now, since we'd both been tested and she was on the pill. Her pussy squeezed me tight as I pushed in slow, inch by inch, until I was buried balls-deep inside. Lifting her right leg higher up for better penetration, I pulled in and out of her, watching her face, desperate for orgasm, desperate for me to give her pleasure, until she shook and begged and writhed beneath me.

"Harder," she gasped, banging her head against the door. "Rougher."

I refused, giving her what she deserved, my adoration and control, so I kept the slow, steady pace, fighting off my own orgasm until I felt her pussy clench around me. At that precious moment, I ground my hips harder against her clit, and she came, screaming my name, milking me dry. I shouted and gave myself up to my own climax, the silky heat of her skin, and musky scent of arousal drowning me, until she slumped downward and I caught her in my arms.

Wrecked and sated, I carried her to the couch and lay down for a few minutes. Her hair spilled across my chest, and her thighs were wet from my come. She snuggled against me, and in that moment, I knew I'd never love anyone the way I did Quinn Harmon, ever again.

"Did you really make pasta, or was that just an excuse to lure me over?"

I laughed, pressing a kiss against her temple. "I really made it. Rigatoni and Newman's sauce. Organic, and proceeds go to charity. Oh, and there's bread, too."

"Sounds so good. But I can't move."

I rolled over, running my hands over her luscious, naked body. Her slim hips and long legs were lithe and strong, her breasts extra sensitive to any wicked thing I wanted to do. And her pussy was heaven, trimmed neatly with a perfect landing strip for my tongue. "I'll serve you. Stay here. Don't put on clothes."

I made her a plate, warmed it up in the microwave, and cut a thick piece of Italian bread. Then I carried it back to her and watched her eat, her gratitude for the simple meal and caring I took making my heart clench. Funny, I'd grown up with private chefs and five-star restaurants, never having to cook in my life. Since I'd moved to Chicago and had to make do on a tight budget, I learned the importance of pasta, clipping coupons, and getting excited over a sale. I was also more satisfied than I'd ever been, finding the food I cooked and paid for the most enticing meals of all.

Right then, I realized I had everything I ever wanted. My one-bedroom apartment sported a worn cream carpet, garage sale furniture, and a tiny bathroom with a leaky faucet. The kitchen had an electric stove, refrigerator that hummed loudly day and night, and cheap linoleum floors with a tiny table and two chairs. The lights were dim, the walls a chipped mud-brown, and my art room was now my living room instead of an entire attic pooled in sunlight.

And I didn't give a shit.

I had Quinn.

That, in my, mind was worth everything.

Would I have changed anything if I had known what lay ahead?

I'd never know.

Chapter Three
Quinn

I GRABBED JAMES'S HAND TIGHT as we wove our way through the diner and headed to my father's favorite booth. I knew it well. I used to pick him up there many times during his drunken days, trying to force coffee down his throat and get him sober for the day. The memory still haunted me, but Dad took pride in staying in that same booth, still fighting his demons. He's been three years clean now, and though I'd never forget the hellish past, I'd moved forward with him.

I reached the booth and leaned over to press a kiss on his cheek. "Hi, Dad."

"Hi, sweetie." He gave James a slight nod, and I tried not to roll my eyes at my father's sudden overprotectiveness. Cracked red vinyl squeaked as we slid into the seat. Familiar sounds and scents swarmed around me; the crackle of bacon, the low hum of morning chatter, the smell of hash browns. The black-and-white checkered floors and ancient juke box in the front gave the place an old Fifties vibe, but lacked the retro coolness to gain the younger crowd. Customers came for a cheap, hearty breakfast, and to recover from hangovers with greasy burgers and strong coffee.

The waitress glided by. She had dark curls, green eyes, and seemed about my father's age. Her gaze rested briefly on my Dad with longing, but he seemed clueless. Finally, she turned to me. "Get you something, hon?"

"The veggie omelet. Coffee, please."

"You got it." James ordered eggs and bacon. The waitress turned to my Dad. "Can I get you anything else?"

"No, thanks."

She seemed about to say something else, but he seemed more interested in staring at James. Finally, she walked away, and I let out an exasperated breath. "Dad, the waitress liked you. Why didn't you talk to her?"

He frowned. "I did talk to her. About my order. You're seeing things."

"What I saw was her making googly eyes at you," I teased. A giggle burst from my lips at the red flush in his cheeks. Dad was attractive, but he refused to date. He always said his one great love had come and gone, and he was fine with keeping himself busy and sober. He did a lot with Alcoholics Anonymous and the New Beginnings Rehab Clinic I wanted to work at. Dad was an attendee and successful graduate. With his tall build, beard, thick, dark hair shot with silver, and blackish eyes, he had a strong presence. People paused when he walked into a room. Another component that made him a great speaker. He commanded attention.

"Let's switch the subject, shall we? How are you kids doing?" he asked in his usual gruff voice. I caught his emphasis on kids as he looked at James. I slid my hand casually over and linked my fingers with James, giving Dad a subtle warning. He still wasn't on board with James moving to Chicago to be with me, but he was civil. He tried. Dad didn't want me to get distracted from my career, hoping I'd go on for my master's degree in social work. James, unfortunately, wanted Dad to like him so bad my heart hurt. I kept telling him to be patient, and with time, Dad would come around, but so far his approval had been slower than Congress.

James shot him a smile. "Good. Art classes are going well. Quinn got another A on her Advanced Psychology exam."

Dad nodded. "That's my girl. Graduate with honors, and it will look damn good for getting that full-time position at the clinic. How's the nursing home?"

I stole a piece of my father's toast. "Same. Still don't like the way some of the residents are treated, but it's not outright abuse. Just a bit of meanness."

"You have a soft heart, Quinn. Keep your eyes open and report anything illegal. I think workers sometimes get burnt out. Another thing you continuously watch for, in yourself and others."

Dad loved to teach. Usually, his words made perfect sense, but sometimes the past reared up, and I got resentful of him telling me what to do. I'd been through Al-Anon and counseling, so I knew those issues would always pop up, but when you spend years taking care of your father and cleaning up his messes, it's easy to get a bit pissed off when he pretends to know everything.

He'd always been a drinker—an alcoholic—but after my mom died there was no barrier between us any longer. I became the parent, and him the rebellious teen child. Dealing with losing mom and cleaning up my father's continued drunken escapades made me a wreck. Sometimes, I felt like I wasn't going to make it. I just wanted to lie down in a ball under a blanket and never get up.

But I did. 'Cause I knew my mom was watching me, and wanted me to succeed. I did everything to make her proud. I wasn't very religious, but I felt her with me most of the time, like this presence wrapped around me in a warm hug. So maybe I was more religious than I thought, or more spiritual.

CHASING ME

It wasn't like believing in ghosts, either. Sometimes, when I had to make a hard decision, I'd clear my mind and ask her what I should do, and most of the times I had my answer.

Dad and I finally mended our relationship after he showed me he could stop drinking, but it took over a year for me to begin to trust him again. Now, we met as equals.

"And what about you, James? Any thought to going back to college?"

James squeezed my hand. "No, Mr. Harmon, I'm trying to carve out a career with my art. The basic program is a year, so we'll see where I'm at then. If I get into the expo in the Spring, I'll have the contacts I need."

"No worries with money?"

I froze. This was the sensitive subject I hated discussing. Even though James was worth millions, he'd decided to stop using his trust fund and refused to take anymore of his parents' money. I was really proud of him, but it was hard to go from the jet-setting life to a small apartment where we really couldn't afford to go out much anymore.

"Trying to make do. I just got a job at Joe's Coffee shop for some extra cash, so that'll help."

I gasped. "You didn't tell me about that!"

James shrugged. "Didn't want to until I got the job. I start Monday."

The waitress came with our food. Dad pointed his fork at James. "Nothing wrong with hard work in any field. We do what we have to."

James smiled, but it seemed a bit lackluster. "Absolutely. Besides, I'll be able to make Quinn those designer coffees she loves."

I tried to eat my omelet, but my stomach was all twisty. Why was I so nervous about him working at a coffee shop? I agreed with my dad. I'd done jobs at all levels and felt proud no matter what it was. But James had already made so many changes. A year ago, he'd been spending money without a care, traveling to exotic places all over the world. Would serving coffee for tips be too much, too soon? "What about the art store that supplies the school?" I asked. "You'd be so good there."

"Competition is stiff," he said, pushing his scrambled eggs around on the plate. "Only a certain amount of spots, and they were already taken. I put in applications all over town, but Joe's was the one to snap me up."

I smiled back at him with encouragement. God, I loved him so much and wanted him to be happy. With me. Here, in Chicago. When he first came, the summer was stretched ahead of us, full of lazy mornings and endless possibilities. We spent hours in bed, limbs entangled, wracked in so much pleasure it should have been illegal. But when we both went back to school, things shifted, and the real world settled in. I was used to it, but every day I watched him struggle, trying to get used to a life he'd never known. Even the sex was beginning to change. He was more in control now. Softer. Like I was fragile, and he put me up on a shelf so I wouldn't break. I'd catch glimpses of the wild lover I adored, but then something changed, and suddenly he was full of control and a bit of distance. Like getting me off was his job, and he wasn't as caught up in the fall. It was frustrating since our lovemaking had always been raw and frantic, pushing me over the edge in a way I desperately needed. I was always too much in my head, and James balanced that part, ripping down my boundaries and forcing me into listening to my body. Now? He was so...careful. Now he rarely had sex with me in any other place but the bed. I thought of our last encounter, when I'd insisted he take me against the door, and shivered. So hot. Yet he'd tried to drag me to the bed, saying I deserved more.

I tried to bring it up, but it was too weird a conversation. I hoped it was a stage, and soon he'd go back to the James that took what he wanted, breaking me down and building me back up through the physical. I ached to see him succeed with his art and want to settle in Chicago with me, happy forever.

You sound like a Stevie Wonder song. How long can he pretend to want the kind of life you have? When he can have anything at his fingertips just by dealing with his parents?

Be quiet. We love each other. Doesn't love conquer all?

Now you sound like MacKenzie belting out her country hits. You're on borrowed time, babe. Enjoy it while you can.

"Shut up."

"What?" my father asked.

James tugged at my hair, his face softening. "She talks to herself a lot," he explained. "Calls the voice her inner bitch. Want me to take her on?"

I grinned. "Nah, I won this round. She's quiet now."

And just like that, my worries drifted away under the sting of his gorgeous blue eyes. I took in his bulk, dressed in jeans and a dark wool sweater that only emphasized all those mouth-drooling muscles. His burnished hair fell sexily into his eyes. From his carved cheekbones, arched brows, and lush, soft lips, he was the type of man women followed with their eyes and crushed on. He had this wicked mischief in his gaze that promised a woman the moon and stars and back again.

And boy, did he deliver that promise.

My father cleared his throat, which meant I'd been staring at James again, so I focused back on my plate.

"What do your parents think of art school, James?" my dad asked.

James stiffened, averting his gaze. "I don't talk much with them, sir. I called my father to let him know, of course, but we don't have much contact."

Dad frowned. "That's concerning. They're your parents. I'm sure they want the best for you. I know if Quinn moved and made a huge career change, I'd like to be kept abreast."

"It's different with James," I interrupted. "He's been on his own for years. His father said it's either college or join him in the family business."

Dad raised his brow. "Sounds fair to me. Responsible."

I squirmed in my seat with annoyance. "Dad, you don't understand the history. James has a right to make his own decisions."

"Not if his parents are paying."

James shoved the plate away and gave a tight smile. "You're right. Listen, I'm sorry, but I have to run. Mr. Harmon, it was good to see you again. I completely forgot I told some of my classmates I'd join them for a painting session."

"James—"

"I'll be back later, and we'll spend some time together."

"But"

He leaned over and pressed a kiss on the top of my head. Threw down a few bills on the table, then walked out of the diner.

Unease slithered through me. "What are you doing?" I hated the almost satisfied look on my father's face. "Talking about his parents upsets him."

"Quinn, I didn't mean to upset the boy. But as a parent, I thought I'd stick up for them. As far as I can see, they've paid for his education, he's dropped out of three colleges, refused to work in the business, and gave them a big screw-you. Does this sound right to you?"

I closed my eyes and fought my temper. "You don't understand the history. What about us? We had our own patches of trouble. How would you feel if some other parent was chiding me for not giving you the proper respect when you didn't deserve it?"

Dad jerked back. Hurt flickered over his face.

Ugh, I hated being bitchy. "I'm sorry, Dad. Forget it. Just don't mention his parents when you see him again. Okay?"

"Fine. Whatever you want. I just want what's best for you. You know that, right?"

I sighed. "Yes, I know. But James is best for me. He makes me happy."

He nodded then grabbed the bills off the table and gave them to me. "Here, breakfast is on me. Give this back to him and tell him I'm sorry."

I smiled, softening. The thing about my father was even when he screwed up, he manned up and admitted it. "Thanks, Dad."

He smiled back and shook his head. "Welcome. Listen, I'll be speaking at a special anniversary meeting on Friday night at AA. Can you come?"

"I think so. Yes."

"Good, it will be nice to have you in the audience for support."

"I'll be there."

We paid the check, hugged, and I started off back to my apartment. The Chicago wind froze my cheeks and stole my breath, but it felt good. Cleansing. I shoved my hands in the pockets of my green pea coat and hoped James was okay. My black boots ate up the pavement, and my mind spun. When we'd first met in Key West, he'd been plain about the truth of his past, calling himself a poor little rich boy. But the pain beneath his words was real and raw. Money didn't buy love or caring, and James's parents barely checked in with him, only wanting him to lead a proper life that didn't embarrass them or put them out. They rarely reached out, and even when James had called them about art school, they'd been cold, telling him he was on his own if he wanted to pursue a ragtag career.

I climbed the stairs, making my way into the brick building located close to the University. My best friend Cassie and I were going to room together at one time, since we weren't rich like MacKenzie, but we both ended up preferring our own space. My studio held all the basics, which I'd made homey with bright afghans, plants, and plenty of books. The futon did double duty as my bed and couch, and the kitchen had a microwave, stove, and refrigerator, with a small countertop. My television was old, not even a flat-screen, but it worked fine, and I was able to afford cable, so that was good enough for me.

I shivered, turned up the space heater, and grabbed my books to do some studying before James came over. We'd spend some quality time together, and maybe I'd wear those sexy red panties I'd been saving for a special occasion.

I pushed away thoughts of sex and James and concentrated on my studies.

Chapter Four
James

I LEFT THE DINER AND HEADED toward the Brush Institute. I'd lied about having a session, but I needed to get my head right and figured working on my project would help.

Fuck. Quinn's father had no respect for me, and I didn't blame him. I couldn't lie. As much as my parents were assholes, I was still the rich kid who'd blown through money and partied nonstop. While Quinn worked her way through college and actually helped people, I'd only helped by financing my friends with unlimited cocktails and holding the most famous parties in Key West.

Who would've thought trying to be a better man would be this so fucking hard?

I hated that Quinn was uncomfortable in front of her dad on my behalf. And working at a coffee shop was hard for me to take. But what the hell? Work was work. Money was money. I'd grit my teeth and deal with it because all steps led to Quinn.

I showed my ID, walked inside, and headed toward my room. The portrait class was basic shit, not helping me at all, but on the weekend the school was quiet, and students were able to come in to use the facilities to work on their projects. I was completing a series of charcoal sketches experimenting with how age changes the face. I'd been obsessed since seeing the picture in some trashy magazine on how a well-known celebrity had changed so much no one seemed to recognize her. Of course, the press went nuts and blamed it on plastic surgery, but studying the planes and lines of her face, I became fascinated by how time can soften and sharpen basic features, especially when combined with changes in lifestyle.

It was a good project to match up with drawing basics so Ava, aka Ms. Goodridge, wouldn't curl her lip and tell me in that frosty tone it was not acceptable for her class. God, I hated her. But I wanted her approval more.

Pathetic.

There wasn't anyone in my room today, so I took a bit of time to prep, setting up my easel and lining up my charcoal pens. I usually liked to work to music, but since school started and that option was taken away, I was getting better dealing with the silence. In a way, it was kind of nice. Forced me to focus and fight through the mental chatter always going on.

I began working, and after a bit, I got into the zone. Always reminded me of that baseball movie I enjoyed with Kevin Costner – *For the Love of the Game*. Clear the mechanism. He'd get in the zone and be able to pitch his game without distractions. When I got to that place, it was like being on my boat, surrounded by water and nothing on the horizon but possibilities. Clean. Pure. Like flying.

My fingers flew, curled, created. I didn't know how long I was at it before my skin began to prickle, and I knew I wasn't alone.

My head turned, and I locked gazes with Ms. Goodridge.

Trying not to startle and be cool, I took in her appearance with neutrality. She looked like a typical artist. She was tall, tall enough to easily be a model, with hip-length straight red hair. She always wore black; skinny black jeans, a black sweater, and black boots. Black, librarian type of glasses. Red lips and heavy makeup. Dramatic, powerful, and a bitch on wheels.

Her face held no expression as she clicked over and studied my work in silence. Sweat broke out on my brow, but I kept cool, refusing to speak before she did. Hell, it was my time anyway, and we weren't in class. She shouldn't even be here, let alone trying to judge me.

"You're still overcompensating," she finally said. The air thickened. "How many times must I tell you, Mr. Hunt? You must first adhere to structure before being able to break it."

Anger shot through me. I clenched my fists. "I do. I did. Look." I pointed to the curve of cheekbone, the strong brush of jaw. "I'm following the rules."

"Not good enough. The width of the eyes and space for the forehead is unbalanced, and not in a good way. You're rushing to get to the good parts, and not taking enough time on foundation. Do you think I've given you art history basics to hear myself talk? Start again, and give me what I've been trying to teach you for six weeks."

She turned on her heel to leave, and I lost it. "What the fuck is your problem?" I asked. "I get that you're trying to teach me, but you don't do this shit to the others. You like insulting me. I didn't bitch when you stuck me in the basic classes to waste my time. I followed the rules time and time again. But I can't seem to satisfy you."

Ah, shit.

I held my breath and waited for her fury. Waited to get thrown out on my ass over my crappy temper issues. Again.

Instead, she tilted her head and stared at me. Her eyes were the lightest green, almost gold, and now they drilled into me as if probing my very soul. A trickle of awareness slid down my spine. What the hell was going on? That look was just...uncomfortable. Not like a teacher to a student. More like a woman to a man. Right? Unless I was just screwed up in the head and imagining things not there.

"Mr. Hunt, I assure you I'm not out to *get you*. I'm here to do my job and push your limits. I think you've had an easy life, and you don't know what to do with the first criticism you've received on something important to you."

I jerked back. Damned if she wasn't right. My art was my heart and soul, other than Quinn, and the idea of failing put me in a cold sweat of fear. Either way, I was already on her shit list, and challenging her wasn't a good idea.

"I'm sorry," I said shortly.

She kept studying me. "Mr. Hunt, do you have a problem with men?"

I blinked. "Huh?"

"Men. It seems you are always drawing women. Now, I know they are probably more interesting due to your gender, but a true artist does not limit himself."

I stared at my portrait. I never really thought of it before, but my subjects were mostly female. "Does it really matter?" I challenged. "They both have similar structure to sketch, which seems to be the point. I'd draw a male just as well as I do a female."

"Again, you refuse to push yourself, Mr. Hunt. We will be having a nude model come in next week to pose. Since it's a male, I'll be looking forward to you proving your theory. For now, I'd advise you to start again, and go back to basics before allowing yourself to stretch boundaries."

I seethed with frustration, having no fucking clue what she was talking about. My fingers curled tight around the pencil, but she didn't seem to care what emotions I was struggling with. The click of her heels resolutely dismissed me as unworthy for a longer conversation. I studied the picture, which I had thought was pretty good, and ripped it to pieces.

Fine. I'd start again. I'd keep going till my fucking fingers were bloody and my eyes crossed if I'd just be able to do one lousy thing that didn't make her lips purse like she just sucked on a damn lemon.

I got back to work.

Hours later, I realized I was late for my date with Quinn. I grabbed my phone, which I'd put on silent, and found three text messages asking when I'd be there. Shit. I quickly texted her to give me thirty minutes, packed up my stuff, and flew back out of the school.

Since my place was close to the school, I showered and changed in record time, and got to her house with two minutes to spare. When she opened the door, she had a cute sulk to her lips I rarely saw. Quinn wasn't the whiney, high-maintenance sort. Another reason why I loved her. Little makeup, casual clothes, honest to a fault, she was a straight-shooter and rarely complained. When she did, I found her spikes in temper hot as hell.

"Sorry, babe." I kissed those gorgeous lips. "I got caught up."

She smelled like everything clean in the world. Cucumber. Cotton. Pure soap with just a hint of floral. I wanted to strip off her clothes and devour her, but I'd promised her an actual date on the town since we'd been working so hard.

"I'm hungry."

"You're pouting. It's adorable."

She gasped. "I don't pout. I'm just starving, like my stomach is eating itself, I'm so hungry."

I laughed. "And you're dramatic. Well, let's go, then. What are we waiting for?"

She grumbled as she donned her coat, pulled a knit hat over her head, and wrapped a scarf around her neck. One thing I learned about Chicago in January? The so-called Windy City froze my balls off. "What are we doing?" Quinn asked.

"Not sure." Funny, in the past, I usually planned elaborate dates. Dinners on my boat, beach cruises, dancing in celebrity clubs. But I loved exploring the unknown with

Quinn, just throwing myself out into the world with her at my side and an adventure before us. I was used to expectations entwined with money. Quinn couldn't have cared less about expensive dinners, and her favorite was a hot dog at the food truck. "Let's go to The Bean and figure it out from there."

"Sounds good. Food first."

I knew the only way to satisfy her appetite was the best damn deep-dish pizza invented. We left the apartment, and I pulled her in tight against me, wrapping myself around her delectable body to protect her from the wind. We'd gotten used to walking everywhere, and I enjoyed living in such an amazing city filled with art, food, and interesting people, even if I missed my boat and the sun occasionally. I never expected Quinn's city to become mine, but in these past six months, I'd made it my own, too.

We finally reached Gino's East and got into a booth, ordering our favorite classic deep-dish with sausage. "Why were you so late?" Quinn asked.

I didn't want to get into it, but owed her the truth. "I was working on my portrait when Ava came in. Let's just say she made it quite clear it sucked. I started over."

She nibbled her lower lip in that sexy way of hers that made me jealous. I wanted to be the one sucking on her lips. "Just because she teaches there doesn't mean she knows what she's talking about," Quinn said fiercely. "Maybe she's a wannabe artist and she's jealous!"

I laughed. Damned if she didn't make me feel good believing in my talent more than anyone else. Quinn never spoke badly about anyone, so this was a sign of her loyalty. "Gonna beat her up for me, baby?" I teased. "My money's on you to take her down."

Quinn rolled her eyes. "Seriously, James, is there anyone else you can talk to at the Brush Institute? The Dean or program coordinator?"

They placed the sizzling pizza on our table. The scent of garlic, sauce, and gooey cheese hit me hard, making me salivate. We dug in with little fanfare and hardly any manners. "Nah, I'm gonna handle this myself. If I have to suffer for the next few months, then I'm done with her. I can take anything she gives me, and now I have something to prove."

"Doesn't she have a say in who displays their work in June?" she asked. "I don't trust her."

That worried me. There was a student exhibition at the end of the year where some high-society art dealers and patrons attended. The Brush Institute had a great reputation with some serious successful artists, and I needed to get there. But I still had time to dazzle, and I wouldn't give up until I did. "Next week I get to sketch a nude male," I said. "I got this."

Quinn giggled. "Can I come with you to make sure?"

"Funny. You're done seeing any other male naked but me."

She batted her eyelashes. "You're enough naked man for me."

"Good. I'll prove it to you again later."

That familiar electricity snapped between us. Her eyes darkened, and I knew she wanted me right then as bad as I wanted her. I wondered if this connection would ever fade between us. It was more intense than anything I'd ever imagined, and I wanted to burn in it. I sucked in a breath and tried to concentrate on my pizza.

"Have you heard from Mac yet?" I asked. One of Quinn's best friends was a famous country star and went on tour with her boyfriend. I knew both Quinn and her other friend Cassie missed her bad, but were really proud of her.

"Not for a few days. I try not to bother her when she's on the road, but I had her pinky promise to check in with me weekly. She gets crazy involved with her music. Cassie and I want to be sure she's okay—we worry."

"Austin's with her."

"I adore Austin, but he's a *boy*. I only trust him so far."

"Reverse chauvinism?"

"Absolutely."

"Guess it's warranted." She stuck her tongue out and finished her pizza.

"Ready for the next part of this amazing date?"

She raised a brow. "There's more? Damn, I would've slept with you on the pizza alone."

"I always knew you were easy." She threw the napkin at me, and I laughed. "Let's go."

We bundled back up and headed toward Millennium Park and Michigan Avenue. The festive lights and crowds, even at the late hour on a blustery day, were one thing I loved so much about the city. Also the amazing epicenter of art. I admitted my snobbery. I'd been to Italy and Paris, viewed amazing works of paintings and sculptures, but there was something vivid and alive in Chicago that was purely American. The Bean rose before us, which was really The Cloud Gate, an elliptical sculpture soaring into the air and reflecting back the city's gorgeous skyline. Within the gated arch of the sculpture, the chambers offered a variety of mirrored surfaces that exploded with images reflected back at the viewer.

I'd kind of fallen in love with the damn thing, seeking it out on many days to study and daydream and sit to ponder. Quinn loved it, too, but I hadn't taken her on this date to see The Bean again. Gripping her gloved hand, I led her to the skating rink without pause.

"We're skating!" She stopped short, staring at the rink where crowds lined up, festive music played on the speakers, and hot cocoa flowed freely. "You hate skating!"

"Not really. It's time to break my virginity, and your dad said you loved to skate."

Her face turned into those stubborn lines I knew well. "James, we don't need to go skating. Let's walk around the park, get a drink at the bar. You don't have to do this."

I leaned down and pressed a hard kiss on her cold lips. "Don't argue. I'm about to skate my ass off, so be prepared for greatness."

"You can skate, then?"

Hell, no. I sucked at skating and most winter sports. Skiing was different. I'd gone with my dickhead friends for years to a luxurious cabin in Vermont, all of us trying to top each other with extreme jumps. There was just something wimpy about doing circles around a rink. Still, I hated to wipe the hopeful look off her face, so I didn't answer, just pulled her into the warm interior and got our skates.

We headed into the rink, and I realized pretty quick I'd made a big mistake.

I had figured I'd bully my way through, make the ice my bitch, and it would all work out. Instead, I became the servant as my legs got tangled up and I hit the ground hard on my bony ass.

Fucking A, that hurt.

"Oh, my God, are you okay?" Quinn knelt down, trying to help me up and making the whole thing worse.

"I'm fine, babe. Just need to warm up. Hey, why don't you do a few laps by yourself, and by the time you get back, I'll be ready to go."

She looked a bit suspicious, but I leaned nonchalantly against the rail, which was my friend and protector, and she bought it. I watched as she pushed off on her skate and glided flawlessly around the circle, weaving in and out of crowds with a graceful beauty I'd never tire of watching.

Her long hair spilled around her shoulders, and her face relaxed. It was as if she went someplace else, her happy place, or something. Fascinating. I'd never really seen her get lost in a hobby she loved. I had to insist she do it more often.

But I guessed first I needed to be able to skate.

I manned up, took a breath, and kept a hand on the ledge as I made my way around, trying to get comfortable on the blades. At one point, a child and I had a war of the rail, but I let her win, tried to push off, and fell back down again.

Motherfucker.

Now pissed off, I threw myself into conquering the wussy sport I used to mock, until my ass was black-and-blue, and I had still only made it halfway around.

Quinn did a twirly thing and stopped perfectly in front of me. "Let me help you. Here, take my hand."

I glowered at her. "I can do this."

Her laugh floated to my ears. "You're so stubborn. And prideful. Okay, listen. Clear your mind, find your balance, and try to shift your weight evenly as you move. Trust your body. It's your mind that makes you fall because you're thinking too hard."

"Sounds like a yoga class rather than a skating lesson."

She made a face. "Come on, try it. I'll skate right beside you."

I gave it a try, cleared my mind, and started forward. I tilted a bit, but instead of panicking, I went with the flow and managed to stay upright for a few beats.

Then went back down.

And so it went. I finally managed to get a halfway decent flow going, and we skated around the rink. Most of the fun was watching her gorgeous ass, all tight and sexy, swing in front of me, her strong legs pumping back and forth as she went faster around the rink. I grew hard, because damned if the woman couldn't breathe without me wanting her. But there was something even more tempting about watching her skate in the cold, her breath making little puffs in the air, her lips curved in a smile, a look of peace on her face.

It hit me like an uppercut that she got cheated. How many times had I wined and dined women who didn't give a shit? With Quinn, the simplest things made her happy, but she deserved more. And here I was, broke, taking her for pizza and skating like any loser guy would. I always thought I was better.

I was wrong.

My buzz leaked away, and what suddenly seemed romantic now felt flat. I had tons of money at my disposal, but instead I was trying to make it on my own to prove something to Quinn and myself. Maybe it would be easier to just use the trust fund. Technically, it was mine anyway. Hadn't I been tortured enough by my parents' lack of interest to make taking the money worth it?

"What's wrong?"

I shook off my thoughts and glanced at her. She frowned, skating backwards like a pro. "Nothing."

"You're lying. When you get upset about something, you purse your lips and your right brow lifts up."

I blinked. "You gotta be kidding me. I don't do that shit." I felt my damn right brow begin to twitch and noticed my lips felt funny. Great. The woman knew way too much about me. "Are you some kind of witch?"

"I just love you."

And with those words, she nailed me good. No one had ever loved me the way Quinn did. Not with such an honest, raw passion and need that made me drunk and giddy.

"You deserve more," I burst out. I stopped skating and swept my hand through the air. "We started off with yachts and mansions on the beach. Now, look at what I've given you. Pizza and a walk in the park in the middle of fucking winter. I'm exactly what my parents always told me. A loser. You should be with a guy who can give you everything you desire."

I waited for Quinn's soft words and defense of my sad state. Instead, the breath whooshed out of me as she took both hands and shoved me full force, so I tumbled back onto the hard ice. I stared up at her, shocked, my ass on fire. "What the hell?" I yelled.

Her dark eyes shot flames. "You're such an asshole!" Her foot, clad in her skate, actually thumped the ice as if she were stamping the ground. "How dare you insult both of us with those lame, whiny statements! I don't need *stuff*. Sure, falling in love with you in Key West was amazing, but do you really think it had anything to do with your fancy house or boat or wallet? Actually, I fell for you in spite of your money. I just want you. The real you, not the guy who hung with his asshole friends, or the boy his parents ignored. I want the passionate, funny, sexy artist who's real with me. Now you got me mad. I better skate it off."

She spun in pure disgust and took off. I lay on the cold ground, staring at the empty space in front of me, while the crowds parted and glanced down to make sure I was okay. Then I began to laugh.

Damn, she was hot. Especially when she got angry. All that quiet energy whipped to the surface and gave off crazy vibes of sex. She saw something inside me I always wanted to believe in, but rarely did, and Quinn never allowed me to doubt. Maybe she was right. Because if she saw all that inside me, there must be something worth fighting for.

I pulled myself up, trying not to wince like a pussy, and skated after her. She was kind of floating in the middle of the ice, making graceful little circles, and I did the only thing I could do and that was to apologize. I grabbed her arm, whipped her around, and kissed her.

Her lips were cold, her tongue was hot, and her mouth was sweet. She kissed me right back, even putting her arms around my shoulders, and I heard the breakout of applause. When we broke off the kiss and looked up, people were clapping and smiling at us, as if we'd starred in some holiday chick flick and I got the girl. Quinn smiled and blushed, and I took a bow, which made them clap harder, and for that perfect moment, I had everything I ever wished for.

When I took her home, I stripped off her clothes with a slow reverence, swearing again not to take her like the animal I was, wanting to give her the adoration she deserved. Running my tongue over her naked body, I swallowed her cries with my mouth, sucked her pussy until she writhed beneath me, crying out my name, but I never stopped, just greedily devouring her musky, honeyed scent that fed me better than cocaine, and felt her come against my tongue.

When I slid inside her tight, pulsing heat, I trembled with the force of a god, her bruised lips still begging me to take her hard, her hands tugging at my shoulders to make me move faster. I fought the violence that Quinn always inflamed and took her slow, measuring my thrusts with perfect precision, making sure she orgasmed first before I felt my balls tighten and I let myself explode, my seed pouring out, my hips jerking in pure fucking ecstasy for endless moments until I thought I'd black out.

We lay in the darkness while I stroked her hair and swore not to fuck this up.

If I'd only listened to my own advice.

Chapter Five
Quinn

I MADE MY WAY INTO THE REC ROOM AT the New Beginnings Clinic, trying to hurry my steps. My father hated lateness, but I'd stopped by Joe's Coffee house first to see James before we parted for the night. Ever since our ice skating rink date, we'd only been able to grab a few quick meals together. Our shifts completely contradicted, which sucked, but we needed the extra money.

I pushed open the door. Dad was speaking, so I snuck to the back row and eased myself into the metal folding chair. The room was structured for AA meetings, Al-Anon, and various workshops offered to help recovering alcoholics. A card table was set up with coffee and donuts. The walls held a few encouraging posters, but that was it.

I rubbed my hands, trying to get warm from the chill, and concentrated on my dad's speech.

"We never got promised fair or easy," he said, looking out into the crowd and meeting everyone's gazes. "We got promised a chance. What we do with it on a moment-to-moment basis is the only thing that matters. We're not gonna be perfect, or get to that holy place we all dream of where suddenly we never want a drink or a hit. The earlier you accept that fact, the easier it'll be. We take it craving by craving, and just like grief and rage and pain, it's always there, ready to come out of the closet. That's why we try to structure our lives so we can take it. A good friend. A family member. Hell, a good night's sleep, or a laugh, or anything that we can cling to that's good and right and makes us happy."

I blinked, remembering Mom and the crippling pain her memory still gave me. Sometimes, I'd wake in the middle of the night, catching her scent, and sob into my pillow when I realized she was really gone. I knew Dad missed her every day, but those years he chose the bottle almost killed me. Like him, though, I got a chance at having a real father in my life when he wanted to get clean, and I was grateful. He was also a gifted speaker. I watched as the crowd of mostly men nodded and murmured things under their breath, faces unshaven, fingers gripped around Styrofoam cups, eyes filled with their own memories and demons. Pride shot through me as Dad finished his speech, and everyone clapped. He caught my smile and winked at me, taking a seat in the front row while the director made a few short announcements.

My phone burst out with the sounds of Jimmy Buffet, and I quickly silenced it. Yep, that was my special ringtone for Cassie and Mac. I scooped it up and checked the group iMessage. Mac. Dammit, I'd thought things were great with her and Austin. Cassie and Ty had already broken up due to his job and constant disappearances, and it had taken a while for Cassie to be okay again.

I broke up with Austin. Remember that article I told you about? The one that said he wanted out of the relationship?

I remembered Mac told me about that strange article claiming Austin wanted to break up with Mac. The paparazzi sucked and lied on a regular basis. I typed out, *Yeah, but it's just the usual tabloid fodder.*

Cassie quickly agreed.

But it wasn't. Austin actually said that stuff. He wants more, and I can't give it to him. I...I saw him with another girl.

Fury shot through me. How dare he screw with my friend. I texted fast. *ASSHOLE!*

Jerk! Cassie threw in. I imagined Mac smiling at our combined rage. *He wants to be free...so I'm going to give it to him.*

I wondered what was really going on. I hated for Mac to also lose the man she loved without a fight. I typed out, *Think about it first.*

But the text quickly popped up on my screen. *It's already done.*

In usual Mac style, she'd made her decision and was staying strong. My heart broke for another friend who'd lost the man she loved. I'd see her and Cassie soon in Key West for Spring Break again, when we all planned to meet up, but would I be the only one left in a relationship?

In that moment, I wondered if James and I were as strong as I thought. Sure, we loved each other, but I was still getting that weird feeling he was trying to distance himself from me. The last time we had sex, he seemed to hold back again, and it was really starting to bother me. The first few months we were together, our physical connection lent an almost carnal, violent twinge I adored. It stripped me bare and refused to let me hide. But once again, he acted like I was a fragile piece of crystal that would shatter if he got out of control.

Ugh. How was I supposed to have that kind of talk? I pictured it. *Umm, babe, the sex is great and so are the orgasms, but can you bruise and bite me a bit more to make sure I know you really want me?*

Only you, Quinn. Can't you ever be happy the way things are?

"Shut up. I'm so over you."

"I'm sorry, I thought we just met. You're over me already?"

I squeaked in distress, and jumped from my seat. Damn, I did it again. My cheeks turned hot as I stared at the man before me, flanked by my dad. He was smiling, and cute in that friendly sort of way that put you at ease right away. Ginger type hair and brown eyes that sparkled, he was nicely built and a few inches taller than my five-eight frame.

"Sorry," I said. "I was kinda talking to my phone. Hi, Dad."

"Hi, sweetheart." He gave me a quick hug. "This is Brian Cardone. I wanted to introduce you both since he'll be working at the clinic. He's the new Assistant Director. Brian, this is my daughter, Quinn."

Brian shook my hand in a firm, warm grip. "Nice to meet you. I hear you're looked upon quite highly here."

I smiled back. "Probably 'cause my father is a bit of a superstar."

Dad shook his head. "Not true. Quinn works harder than most, and when she graduates this Spring, we're hoping she'll be able to get a full-time position."

Brian looked intrigued, studying my face for a while. "Well, we'll have to see how we can make that happen, won't we? The clinic needs more people like you. Been with us for a while now. Most quit after six months, not able to hack it."

I shifted on my feet. I always hated being the center of attention, but I wanted a job at the rehab on my own credentials. I loved working at the senior citizen home, but my heart told me I belonged at the clinic, working with alcoholics like my father. I pulled myself to full height and met his gaze full force. "I'm dedicated and want to make a difference here. I believe I can."

He nodded. "Confident, too. I like that. Contact my office for a one-on-one appointment, Quinn." He pressed a card into my hand, lingering a bit. "Call me."

"I will." My skin prickled as he refused to break eye contact, but then he looked up at my dad and I figured it was my imagination. I pegged him around his early thirties, and a total business professional. He'd never be interested in me in that capacity.

My father was beaming when Brian walked away, and seemed more excited than me. "Quinn, he's going to be amazing for us. He has a vision and comes highly recommended from a rehab back in Florida."

I raised my brow. "And he moved here? It's so cold out my nose almost froze off."

"Better opportunity for him. He's settling in, but it wouldn't be a bad idea to offer to show him around. Hard to be in a new city."

"We'll see. I don't want to get too personal if he's going to be my boss."

I saw the calculated gleam in my father's eyes and knew what was going on. He didn't like James, and wanted to see me with a man he believed to be more my type. "Being nice and perhaps becoming friends isn't a big deal. Think about it. He seemed to like you."

"Dad. I love James."

He waved a hand in the air. "Sure. Where is he tonight?"

"At the cafe."

My father didn't respond for a few moments. "Quinn, did you ever really think of what could happen to you two if this art thing doesn't work? He has no education. No skills. He's almost twenty-five. What type of future do you plan on?"

My heart beat, but I remained calm. "A future together is all I want. He'll succeed because he's amazing, and I believe in him. Now, I don't want to talk about this anymore."

"Fine by me. Let's grab a bite to eat."

We stopped and chatted a bit with the other attendees, but my father's words kept flashing in irritating neon. We'd only been together about eight months, and lived for the moment. Sure, we were deliriously happy, but would we have to start thinking seriously past the moment and make hard decisions? Were we ready to handle the hard stuff, beyond our connection, and make it work?

Yes. Because our love was special and real. As my father said, life wasn't supposed to be easy, but if we were committed to each other and worked hard, everything would work out.

Chapter Six
James

"JAMES! WHERE'S THE cafe mocha latte with skim?"

"Coming!" I ground my teeth together, wiping down the disgusting tables with a rag, then hurried back behind the counter. The fucking beast machine with its intimidating silver sheen, dials galore, and burning steam that had already torn some of my skin off, mocked me, waiting to screw with me for the millionth time.

Joe's was wildly popular with the college crowd, who were both low tippers and slobs, the worst combination. It had taken me a while to get into the routine of working coffee, and I gotta admit I had it all wrong. Trust me, being behind the counter is a different experience. I remember how many times I'd waltz in, order a bunch of designer coffees, complain about the wait, and stroll out without another thought.

Karma was a bitch.

I grabbed the cup, wiped my sweaty brow with the back of my arm, and began working the bitch machine, trying to get the steps right without visiting the hospital with second-degree burns. I got this one right, though the foam was low, but I threw a lid over it and got it to the guy in the leather coat with his designer glasses. His gaze flicked over me like I was an uninteresting insect, and he flipped his change into the big glass jar that read *WE LOVE TIPS*. The few quarters clinked against the sides and fell into the mostly empty jar. He wore Italian gloves, a cashmere scarf, and smelled of Clive Christian cologne. Bastard.

My temper inched a few levels higher, but I swore to keep it together. Reality sucked, but I needed to think of the big picture. Get into the art show, make some contacts, and get the hell out of this dead-end job. Check.

The next hour flew as I made coffee, cleaned tables, and heated up pieces of quiche, placing a sprig of parsley on it in an effort to make it look gourmet. My pansy T-shirt marking me a proud Joe's employee stuck to my chest. The shop was stuffy and hot, and being around the endless steam didn't help my smell. I wondered how Quinn was enjoying her night.

"James Hunt!"

I turned at the sound of a familiar voice. My heart sank to hell itself when I stared into my old friend's face. "Rich? What the hell are you doing here?"

Rich and Adam had been my best buddies for most of my life. We grew up together with our rich parents, tearing through our trust funds and traveling the world spending our money. Rich had been with me in Key West when I first met Quinn, and bet me I couldn't bed her within the week. When I came clean and chose her, Adam and Rich weren't too happy about my decision, and we had a huge fallout. Hadn't talked since. I had to admit I didn't miss them much, either. Distance made me realize what assholes they were, and how I became one of them when we hung together. I hated who I became with them, and rarely gave them much thought.

Rich's gaze flicked over my dirty T-shirt, sweaty face, and hands holding a cup of coffee. A vicious delight gleamed in his dark eyes, and I knew I was about to get shit. "I flew in to attend the museum banquet. Dad's on the board, and you know how he likes to keep up appearances." His lip curled. "Speaking of appearances, is this what love brought you to, buddy? Adam and I were wondering why we haven't seen you around. Now I know why. We prefer the country clubs and the party scene. Not the coffee shops."

I rolled my eyes, trying to act cool though I wanted to punch him in the mouth. "Whatever, dude. Take your shot, but you'll still be the asshole in the end."

He laughed. "Still arrogant, huh? Always were. It's nice to see you come down a level or two. Hey, maybe you and Quinn will get married. Get a little apartment together. You can work the coffee shop, she can waitress, and you'll live happy ever after. Eat mac and cheese, pop out a few brats, and wake up one day ready to blow your brains out. Sound good?"

I lowered my voice. "Fuck you. You never cared about anyone but yourself. You use people, have no real friends, and wouldn't know something real if it bit you in the ass."

He smirked. "Yet I'm still rich and happy. And you're not."

I held back, trying to breathe, when one of the other servers came over. "You being helped, sir?"

Rich grinned. "Not yet. I want a caramel macchiato with skim, no whip. I'd like this man to take my order, please."

"Of course." The server walked away, giving us an odd look, and I realized Rich would win this round no matter what. He'd caught me at my lowest, and it didn't matter if I had gotten the girl. I pictured him calling Adam, them having a few good laughs at my expense and gossiping about me to the rest of their crew until it got back to my parents.

Fuck it. Fuck them. All of them.

The old me would've shot over the counter and pounded his face. The new me turned away, went to the machine, and got his order. I slid it over the counter, keeping my face expressionless. "That'll be $4.57," I recited.

CHASING ME

Rich gave me a five. "Keep the change, buddy. Maybe that'll help you out. You and your noble intentions."

His laugh mocked me as he turned and strode out without a backward glance. I tried to push him to the back of my mind and finish my shift, reminding myself I was the one who was happy with my new life.

But his words still burned like a rash I couldn't get rid of.

When I got to my crappy apartment, I showered and texted Quinn I was home. The quiet was conductive to brooding, so I sat and waited for her to answer me, but when a few minutes went by I knew she'd fallen asleep. I went to the small dorm-type refrigerator, cracked open a Coors Light, and drank.

I thought of Rich laughing with Adam and telling his father how far James Hunt had fallen. I'm sure my parents would catch wind of my new job skills, and call with a humiliated command to use my damn trust fund and go back to Florida where I belonged.

But I didn't belong there anymore. I didn't belong anywhere.

Except with Quinn.

I finished my beer, grabbed my phone and keys, and headed back out the door. Toward her apartment. Head tucked against the needle-like wind, I reached her place in record time, slid my key into the lock, and let myself in.

She was asleep in the bed. One leg tangled in the sheets, dark hair spilling over the white pillow, little snores that she swore she never did emitting from her lips. My gut twisted, and I slowly took off my clothes, climbing into bed with her. She was warm and smelled clean and pure, and my dick hardened to get inside of her and forget everything but what she made me feel. I woke her slowly, my mouth sipping her at her plump lips, until she gave a catchy moan that got me more aroused, and I delved deep into her mouth, savoring her taste.

She arched, entwined her arms behind my head, and gave it all back. Completely surrendering to me, even in sleep. I felt bigger than fucking Superman, and a bit of my control broke. I got rougher, stronger, pinning her to the mattress and parting her thighs, rocking my erection between her legs. I was ready to surge inside and bury myself deep.

Her eyes opened. Pupils dilated, drugged, she whispered my name. "James."

"You're mine. Just mine. Forever."

I delved my fingers into her pussy, loving the way she clenched around me tight, as if refusing to let me go. I curled my index finger the way she liked it and went straight for her G-spot, which made her cry out and launch halfway off the bed.

"Say it," I commanded. The beast inside me roared for me to take her hard and make sure she never forgot, but I tried to keep it together. "Now."

"I'm yours. Forever. Oh, God, gonna come—"

"Come now," I whispered fiercely, biting her cherry-red nipple at the same time I flicked her clit with the pressure I knew got her every time. "Now, Quinn."

"Oh, God, yes!"

She came hard, shuddering under my grip, and I lifted my head from her breast to watch her face. Possession beat in waves inside me. Swearing she'd never be in another guy's arms, I surged forward and buried my dick deep inside her.

I threw back my head and shouted her name. Caught on the edge of losing my control, I thrust inside her over and over, just barely hanging on to my sanity as I felt her come again over my dick, bathing me in her arousal, falling into me as deep as I fell into her.

We collapsed together in a tangle of limbs, breathing hard, and she rolled over into the position she loved, tucking her head into my chest. My heart began to slow, and the elusive peace I always sought with art settled over me, making me realize everything was right as long as she was in my arms.

"Tough night?" she murmured huskily.

I laughed a bit. "You have no idea. Rich came into the place."

"Rich, your asshole friend from Key West?"

I laughed again. Quinn rarely cursed, but when she did it was pretty spectacular. "Yep. He was in town for some banquet and thought he'd stop in for a coffee to torture me."

She rolled over and caught my chin. Her dark eyes were worried. "He's scum, James," she said. "I'm sure he gave you a hard time and tried to make you feel like crap."

Quinn didn't know the half of it, but I wasn't about to tell her how his taunts affected me, even when I didn't want them to. Seemed I was always struggling with my worth as a man. But I was tired of being a fucking whiner. *Poor little rich boy*, the voice inside me mocked. Over a million dollars at my disposal whenever I got bored of playing the working stiff, while people out there struggled with jobs every day to support their families and had no blanket policy. I disgusted myself.

"Uh-oh, he did get to you." Quinn peered into my face. "He's pissed because you took off and won't finance his fun anymore."

I laughed. Damned if she wasn't right. My friends loved to have me around to throw the big-ass parties and always foot the drinking bill. "He left me a few quarters for a tip," I teased.

She kissed me. "He's a dickhead. I hope we don't see him when we go back to Key West."

Oh, yeah. We'd planned to go back to the Keys during Spring Break, meet all her girlfriends, and celebrate our year anniversary. Now? I had the big art show to worry about, and finding enough money to fly us over, stay at the Coves, and make sure my ex-friends didn't bother us. Great.

"Maybe we should drive," I threw out. "Could be an adventure."

She arched a brow. "Are you kidding? It would take too long. Listen, Mac already said she'd put us all up at the Coves if you're worried about money."

No. Fucking. Way. I wouldn't have her country-star friend, as sweet as she was, paying my bills along with my girlfriend's. For God's sake, last year, Quinn had been sleeping in my mansion. I'd find a way.

"I got it covered," I said smoothly. "I don't want you to worry about the trip. Okay?"

She frowned, but she finally smiled, flipped over, and started pressing kisses over my chest. My muscles clenched, and I became rock-hard again. I tangled my fingers in her long hair and watched her as she made her way to my erection, looked up my body, and gave me that look. The look that could shoot me straight to heaven in a single moment. The look that told me she was all mine.

"Quinn?"

"Shut up, baby. I think we've done enough talking."

She opened her mouth, took me in one long, smooth, hot swallow, and I closed my eyes in ecstasy.

Dear God, I loved this woman.

Chapter Seven
Quinn

I SAT IN BRIAN'S OFFICE, MY legs crossed in my proper black pants, boots, and white lace top. I tried not to fidget as he spent long moments going over my file, which I had brought to show I was organized and prepared. It contained not only a résumé, but letters of recommendation, my current GPA and student records, and testaments of all the people I'd worked with in the past, including referrals from the senior citizen home. I knew it was impressive, and a way to get to the next level beyond the newcomers. I just had to make sure I remained cool, competent, and in control. Those qualities were important to social work or counseling sessions, since emotions ran high and hot on a regular basis.

Brian looked up, pushed the folder away, and smiled. I tried not to jerk at the brilliance in that smile, recognizing he was basically a friendly, happy person who seemed quite satisfied with his life. I knew that was a stretch assumption when I didn't even know him, but I had instincts about people.

"I'm impressed," he said finally, leaning back in his chair.

"Good. That's the reaction I was seeking."

He laughed and tapped his pen casually against the edge of the desk. "Are you too good to be true? It's rare I see someone enthusiastic, with businesslike skills and capabilities this young. Why do you want to dedicate your life to being with a bunch of alcoholics? A pretty, vibrant woman like you?"

I didn't take offense. Just answered the question. "You know my father's story. But this isn't an attempt to make sense out of alcoholism or gain forgiveness for something I don't understand. I worked through a lot of my issues. Went to therapy. Al-Anon. I just have this thing inside me that's only truly satisfied when I'm helping others. Call it the nurturer personality, or maybe I'm an old soul who came back to right some past wrongs. I'm not sure. I just know who I am, and I accept it. Does that make sense?"

Something burned bright in his dark eyes, a gleam of understanding and something much more dangerous. His fingers clenched around the pen, and he gave a jerky nod. "Yeah, it does make sense. Listen, Quinn, I'm setting up a special program for people like you who I'm looking to hire full-time. Problem is, it's demanding. Three nights per week, and I know you also work at the nursing home and have classes. We'll be doing things I've seen in other rehabs which I'd like to implement at New Beginnings, and I'm only taking five people in. I want you to be one of them. Are you interested?"

"Yes." I never hesitated. I knew my schedule was tight, but I wanted this and felt it could be the turning point I needed. I had so much I wanted to be able to give to the residents. Not dreams of unicorns and rainbows and perfect days. I didn't believe in that anymore. Just hope and hard work.

"Good." He shuffled through his desk and handed me a thick packet. "Those are the forms to fill out and get back to me. We start this week."

I nodded. I'd make it work. I couldn't wait to tell James, and though it would be less time we spent together, I knew he'd be supportive. I rose from the chair.

"Quinn?"

"Yes?"

"Are you free for lunch?"

I blinked. Stared. Was he asking me on a date? Or was this business? I felt myself blushing. "I'm, well, I mean, I have to tell you, I—"

"Have a boyfriend?" he interrupted.

I bit my lip, but he didn't look upset, just thoughtful. "Yes."

"Understood. I'm sorry. I didn't mean to make you uncomfortable. I just enjoy speaking with you and wanted to pick your brain a bit."

"Oh." So, it was more about colleague-to-colleague? That, I could handle. He didn't give off any of those weird vibes like he wanted to use his higher position to get favors, or dangle this program in the hopes of dating me. He was passionate about his work, and his personality seemed to fit mine. One worker bee easily recognized the other. "I wouldn't mind grabbing a burger and discussing some things." That felt safe.

"Perfect. We can go right down the street." He grabbed his coat and ushered me out the door, heading toward Rose's Pub, which was known for their gourmet fries. "How's school?"

I wrinkled my nose and tightened my scarf around my neck. Our steps easily matched each other's. "Fine. The last semester is the easiest. I just have to finish up a few projects and keep my A's intact."

"Ah, an overachiever. I'm the same way. I remember when I was in the University of Florida, and I got food poisoning a day before my final exam. The professor was hardcore, so I showed up with practically an IV in my arm and took it."

"Got an A?"

"Of course."

I laughed. We got settled into a booth, ordered two burgers, fries, and Cokes, and settled in. "What made you want to get into counseling?" I asked curiously.

"Same as you. My mom was an alcoholic. I was the oldest, so I took care of her. Co-dependence issues galore. Got fed up, got educated, and gave her tough love. She was not one of the lucky ones, though. Refused to do rehab, so I ended up losing her."

My heart hurt for him. "I'm so sorry."

He gave a half-smile without humor and shrugged. "It's okay. Part of who I am was because of the experience. I was focused on saving everyone else for a while, but now I've balanced out a bit. I just want to offer the best programs I can and let the individual decide if they want to work it. Make sense?"

He gazed directly into my eyes, and I felt my skin tingle. A shared emotion passed between us, as if we recognized ourselves in each other. So strange. Though he was older, I was already an ancient soul, so we were almost evenly matched. I broke the gaze and sipped my Coke. "Makes perfect sense. Exhausting sometimes, isn't it?"

"Yes. But what's the alternative? Mediocrity?"

I smiled. "Maybe. Tell me about your plans for New Beginnings."

The waitress brought our burgers, and we dug in. "I want to add another level to the program. There are a lot more experiments in holistic health, meditation, yoga, et cetera that we only touched on. I'm hiring a brand-new coordinator to run the extra programs, which will extend the regular term by another week."

I frowned. "What about insurance? Most residents want to work the program and get back out. Many can't afford to stay longer."

CHASING ME

His face reflected admiration at my question. "Already working on that, and it's almost approved with some companies. For the others, I'm looking at doing a work-study program in order to get them to stay. Give them incentives. It's a way to reach a bit deeper into the mental blocks alcoholics have."

I'd done classes with holistic techniques and found them favorable. Many alcoholics were quite brilliant, with no way to settle their mind other than looking for another hit. This was a positive way to give them new skills and alternatives. "It's brilliant," I said simply. "I think it would work well at New Beginnings. Tell me more."

We ate our burgers, and he talked animatedly about the ins and outs of the program. I got caught up in his excitement, and realized how alike we were. I was a fixer, nurturer, and enjoyed stability.

Like Brian.

I didn't care, though. I kind of liked who I was, though sometimes I was way too shy and intimidated and felt like the world was spinning out of my control, which I hated. But James balanced me in a way I'd never experienced before. As if by allowing me to feel things so deeply, he'd provided an outlet that gave me more peace than I'd ever had.

Or maybe it was just the multiple orgasms.

I smiled at the thought.

"Now, that was something interesting. What were you thinking about?"

I ducked my head and fumbled with the napkin. Damn, this was awkward. "Umm, nothing. Just planning how to make sure I'm hired."

He leaned back in the booth. The lights gleamed in his ginger hair, and his dark eyes sparkled. He was really handsome in an understated way. Different from James's intense, sexual looks that always made my tummy drop to my toes. No, Brian gave me a settled, happy feeling. Like I wanted to remain around him, talking. "I have a feeling you can get whatever you put your mind to." His lip curled a bit. "Tell me about the boyfriend. In love?"

I shifted in my seat. "Yes. We met last year in Key West on Spring Break. He moved here this past summer."

Brian lifted a brow. "Moved for you, huh? That is serious. What does he do?"

"He's an artist. Goes to school at the Brush Institute."

"Great place. Must be talented."

"He is."

Brian's eyes darkened. He leaned in just a bit and lowered his voice to an intimate pitch. "Then maybe he's worthy of you."

A strange intensity built between us, and I shook my head to clear it. "He is," I said firmly.

"Good."

More staring. Time to leave. I grabbed my purse and placed some money on the table. Suddenly, his hand shot out and entwined with mine. At the touch of his skin over mine, I gasped and jerked back. He studied my expression and slowly pushed the bills back toward me.

"My treat."

"But I—"

"Put your money away, Quinn." His order allowed me no recourse, so I shoved the cash back into my purse and thanked him. I was embarrassed at my lame reaction to a simple touch, but he immediately put me back at ease. We chatted a bit as we left, and I was laughing at one of his jokes about overachievers when I pushed open the door.

And ran straight into James.

"Quinn?" His hands held me hard. Those aqua-blue eyes narrowed as he caught sight of Brian right behind me. Uh-oh. James was known to be extremely jealous and possessive. It was one of the sexy elements that made our relationship exciting, but right now, I needed him to be cool. I jumped right into introductions before he could ask the question.

"James! What are you doing here? This is Brian. He's the new assistant director of New Beginnings." I emphasized his title and hoped he'd get my subtle meaning.

He nodded and stuck out his gloved hand. "Nice to meet you, Brian," he said stiffly. "I'm James. Quinn's boyfriend."

Brian flicked his gaze over James, seeming to catch the undercurrent of warning in his tone. I almost groaned at the pissing match beside me. Men were so weird.

"Nice to meet you, James," Brian said pleasantly, shaking his offered hand. "Quinn was just telling me about you. Says you're an artist."

"That's right." To me, James said, "I was heading to the clinic to let you know I need to stay late at the studio tonight."

"Oh, that's okay. I have an essay to write."

"Fine. Need a ride back to school?"

"Sure, thanks." I turned to Brian, thanked him for lunch, and we said our goodbyes. James was quiet as we made our way toward the car. When I finally slid into the seat and buckled up, I turned to face him. "How was Joe's?"

His jaw clenched. "A real blast. How was your lunch?"

I studied him for any undercurrents of sarcasm, but he seemed sincere. I let out a breath. I was really being ridiculous by expecting him to be jealous just because I had lunch with a male business associate. I guess announcing I belonged to him set up the ground rules between men. "Great. Brian's implementing a new program he wants me to be part of. We were discussing it. I'll be really busy for the next few weeks. He only takes five people in, and I'm one of them."

"Quinn, your schedule is already overbooked. Between school and two jobs, do you have time for this? I don't think it's a good idea."

I raised my chin. "This is important. I think it'll put me in a good spot to get that permanent position once I graduate. I can do this."

He muttered under his breath and squealed into a parking space. Shoving his fingers through his thick hair, he whirled around to face me. "We barely see each other as is. How many more days will you be gone?"

"Three nights per week."

"Fuck."

"I want to do this!"

"Fine. Do it, then."

We stared at each other in furious silence. Long moments passed. The sound of students laughing and walking onto campus echoed through the closed windows. I finally reached out to touch him. As usual, his touch electrocuted me, burning my skin and making me ache to be surrounded by him, his scent, taste, and voice my overwhelming obsession. He felt it, too, because he leaned over the seat and pressed his forehead against mine, his fingers cupping my cheeks.

"Don't be mad," I whispered.

"I'm frustrated," he admitted. "I miss you, and there's all this shit going on all the time. I'm afraid you're going to burn out, baby."

I pressed my thumb against his delicious, full lips, stroking the bottom in a way I know he liked. "I know, but this is important to me."

He groaned and instead of answering, then took my mouth in a hard kiss, slipping his tongue deep inside. I arched up, and his hand twisted in my hair to hold my head still. I thrilled to the demand of the kiss, the spark of his passion heating my blood and making my pussy wet. I ached for him to climb on me right now, yank down my pants, and slide inside me, his gorgeous, big cock thrusting in and out until he gave me that orgasm I wanted with my last breath.

Instead, he broke the kiss, panting a bit, eyes wild, and jerked back. "Okay."

Disappointed, I realized the old James wouldn't have cared about anything but fucking me. Now, he seemed to analyze every move and decision regarding our relationship, and I didn't know what to do about it.

He gave a lopsided smile. "Call you tonight."

I waited for another kiss, but he kept his distance. I forced a smile back and opened the car door. "Love you."

"Love you, too."

The words soothed me as I walked to my class.

Chapter Eight
James

I GLANCED AT MY WATCH AND quickened my pace. I had a rare opportunity to meet Quinn at the art store. I had to buy a shitload of art supplies, and she had time to run over to meet me for lunch.

I tried to be happy, but I had to admit my patience was running out. Two weeks had already passed since she took on the extra workload. We were dealing with conflicting schedules, and barely enough time for a quickie. With her sporadic night shifts at the nursing home, the clinic, and regular schoolwork, I felt guilty interrupting her sleep. The distance between us was frustrating the hell out of me.

I turned the corner, and she was waiting outside the supply store. Dressed in her apple-green coat, wool hat pulled tight over her ears, she stomped her feet for warmth and caught sight of me.

The joyous smile that curved her lips stilled my damn heart. And just like that, I wasn't mad anymore. Her lips were cold and her cheeks rosy red as she lifted her head up for a kiss. "Baby, why didn't you wait inside?" I asked.

"I like to watch you walk."

I shook my head, laughing, and pushed her inside the store. "You know just how to butter me up. Add a deep-dish pizza for lunch, and I'll do anything you want."

She bit her lip, eyes full of apology. "James, I'm so sorry. I only have fifteen minutes before I need to get back."

And then I was mad again. "Are you kidding me? I haven't seen you since Monday. You don't even have time to eat?"

"Brian brought in a special consultant for a presentation. We're grabbing lunch while we work."

Brian. Again. Seemed his name was brought up a lot lately, and though I hated being a fucking whiner, I suddenly felt like an annoying demand in her busy schedule. I reached for patience and tried to control myself. "How about tonight, then?"

"I have a paper, but I'll be done early. Come over after you're done at the studio."

I let out a sigh. I wanted to see her, but her schoolwork was vital. "No. If you need to do your paper, that's more important."

She blinked and reached up, grabbing my face and kissing me hard. "I love you, James Hunt," she whispered. "Come over. I swear my paper is practically done, and you'll give me a great incentive."

Her clean scent teased my senses, and suddenly I was hard and ready to go. I gritted my teeth and tried to get myself under control. Finally, I'd have her naked, laid out in my bed, ready to give herself up to every bad, dirty, lewd thing I wanted to do to her body. "Oh, I'll give you an incentive, all right." I bit her plump lower lip in warning, and she gave a tiny squeal. "You're gonna beg me to get off. Maybe I'll give it to you, maybe I won't."

Her pupils dilated, her breath came out choppy, and I knew she was wet and aching for me. I was about to say to hell with it, back her into the corner, and push my fingers into her pussy.

"Can I help you with something?" a voice interrupted. A guy wearing a store uniform looked at us with pure disapproval.

Quinn blushed and jumped away. "No, thank you."

"Actually, I need some supplies. I have a list here." I took it out of my pocket and handed it to the guy.

He looked happy he'd get a sale rather than a peep show. "I'll get this right away, sir." He disappeared down the deep aisles, and I laughed at Quinn's face.

She hit me in the shoulder. "You're so bad. Do they have any of those artistic greeting cards here?"

"In the back."

"I'll be right back. It's Jessica's birthday, and I forgot to pick one up."

"Meet me over here. I have to look at some different brushes." She nodded, and I watched her gorgeous rear swing back and forth before she disappeared. Grinning, I headed over to the brushes, and began picking them up and discarding different ones.

"You want to make sure they're extra stiff."

The husky voice rolled close to my ear. I jerked, turning around, and came face-to-face with Ava. She was dressed in her usual black ensemble. Her hair fell loose today, a dramatic red that matched her painted lips. Those green eyes were filled with amusement and a touch of something else. Hunger? No.

I kept my tone formal. "Hello, Ms. Goodridge."

Her brow rose. "We're not in class, James. Ava will be fine."

I didn't answer. Shifting my feet, I tried casually to bring some distance between us since she seemed super close, her head bent toward mine as if we were holding an intimate conversation. Her lips curved in a half-smile. "Stocking up?"

"Yeah. My brushes are kind of shot."

CHASING ME

She reached past me. Her arm grazed my chest, and she clasped her fingers around the brush I held. The breath got stuck in my lungs at the deliberate touch. "As I said, the stiffer the brush, the more it holds its shape and gets the job done. Of course, I can work with any brush. It's just a matter of coaxing the right pleasure from it."

Holy. Shit. Was I freaking out, or was she actually giving me a sexual innuendo? I kept silent, afraid to open my mouth, and her low laugh rumbled in my ear. Very slowly, she guided her hand back and rubbed my shoulder. "I've never known you to be so quiet, James. Cat got your tongue?"

I hated her manipulations. She hated my guts, and now she wanted to play head games? WTF? "I've never known you to be so...nice."

"I can be very nice. Maybe we should discuss it sometime."

"Okay, I'm done. Isn't this card pretty— Oh, I'm sorry." Quinn's voice interrupted the psycho conversation, and I immediately jumped to the right so Ava's hand was off me. Quinn looked back and forth between us with curiosity. "Hi, I'm Quinn."

"My girlfriend," I added quickly.

Ava reached over and shook her hand. "Ava Goodrich. James's art teacher at the Brush Institute."

Uh-oh. Quinn's eyes widened, and suddenly she looked like a wet cat, all pissy and ready to spit. Her voice cooled. "Yes, James has mentioned you."

Ava looked almost delighted. "I'm sure he has. James is an excellent artist. Sometimes it's hard as a teacher to push my students in the proper direction, but I think he has raw talent that's quite extraordinary."

Quinn's mouth dropped open. So did mine. "That's what I'm constantly telling him," Quinn said, her voice warming.

"It's a difficult business. But I'm sure he has the passion needed to succeed."

Quinn looked delighted at Ava's compliments. I stared at my teacher hard, knowing there was something else going on. Ava beamed out a bright, fake smile. "It was lovely to meet you, Quinn. James, I will see you in class."

She turned on her high black boot and left the store. Quinn gave a squeal and hugged me. "She said you have raw talent! Maybe that's why she's being so hard on you! She wants to push you because you're the best."

I wanted to tell her about the way she touched me and the things she said, but Quinn looked so happy and proud, I shut my mouth. Maybe tonight, I'd give her the full story, and we could talk. Quinn chattered nonstop as we paid for our stuff. "So, I'll come over tonight, right?" I asked. "We'll have a quiet night."

"I can't wait," she whispered, pressing a hard kiss to my lips. "Gotta go."

I watched her until she vanished around the corner. I don't know why I had a funny feeling in my gut that something bad was gonna happen. But I brushed it off, figuring we'd talk and reconnect later tonight.

If only I'd listened to my initial instincts.

Chapter Nine
Quinn

I GATHERED UP MY NOTEBOOK, exhausted but buzzing from the amazing session. I'd learned more about getting patients to open up and using guided meditation techniques to ease them through the process. The research numbers were impressive, and Brian was really focused on retaining this extra program at New Beginnings.

Rolling my neck around to ease my sore muscles, I thought of a long, relaxing evening with James and grabbed my jacket. Maybe I'd get him to give me a massage. First food. Maybe sex, then food, then massage. At this point, I just needed to get myself home quick.

I popped my head into Brian's office. He was always the last one to leave and the first one here in the morning. I admired his dedication and the way he stood side-by-side with his staff. "Night," I called out.

"Quinn? Got a sec?"

I stood in the doorway. "Sure. What's up?"

He rubbed his forehead. His ginger hair was all messy, and his face looked tired. "Any of the rest of the crew here?"

I shook my head. "No, I'm the last one. Did you need something?"

"I know you've been working nonstop, but I've got a new intake coming in. I could use a hand, and it would be great training. But if you're tired or have schoolwork, I understand."

I bit my lip. Damn. I was torn. I craved seeing James, and I had the paper to finish. Of course, the paper should only take an hour. "Do you know how long it will take?"

"About an hour, start to finish. I'll order some food in." He studied my expression for a moment, then waved his hand in the air. "No, forget it, Quinn. You're pushing too much. Go home. Take a night off."

I wanted this full-time job bad. If I demonstrated willingness to take on extra work and be a team player, I would have a step up on the competition. I took off my jacket and smiled. "I'm staying. I can work on my paper when I get home. It only needs editing."

"You sure?"

"Yes."

He smiled back at me, relieved. "Thanks, Quinn, I appreciate it. You like Chinese?"

"Sounds great. Let me just send out a quick text, and I'll be ready."

I grabbed my phone and walked into the hallway. I knew James wanted to spend some quality time, but I could still get home at a decent hour. I quickly texted him I needed to skip dinner, but to wait for me at home. I told him I'd be there by eight.

Praying he wouldn't be too pissed, I slid my phone back into my pocket and headed inside. "He mad?" Brian asked.

I laughed. "Nope, he understands."

"Good." Brian grabbed a stack of forms. "Pull a chair up, and let's start."

We went over the intake forms, making some changes due to the new programs Brian wanted to implement, then met with the patient. His name was Sam, and he was in his sixties. Gray hair, rough beard, bloated cheeks, beer belly. He gave off the desperate, angry vibe I'd seen from long-term alcoholics who didn't think they'd ever stop, but were tired of living in the gutter. I watched the way Brian dealt with Sam, balancing the fine line of support with tough love. We spent a long time with him, and I realized it was one of the best intakes I'd ever been involved in. Even in just that hour, I learned a lot.

When Sam was settled, we got back to his office, and the Chinese food was laid out in cartons. My stomach rumbled loudly. Brian laughed. "I know. As long as you don't care, I say let's ditch the plates and dig right in."

I collapsed into the chair, grabbed a box of lo mein, and dug out a plastic fork from the paper bag. "Done." He passed over a Diet Coke can, and we ate in happy silence, slurping noodles and savoring the salty spiciness of garlic sauce.

"You're amazing with the patients," I said in between bites. "It's like you know what they need right at the perfect time."

He took a sip of his soda. "Lots of practice. Studying. It doesn't come overnight, but I have to tell you, Quinn, you have a knack. People respond to you."

I shrugged. "I was always the one my friends came to," I explained. "They'd tell me their secrets. I think they knew I could be trusted."

He shook his head. Those light brown eyes turned serious. "It's more than that. You actually care. There's this vibe inside of you that makes people want to be close to you. Makes you feel safe."

Startled, I looked up. Our eyes met and locked. A current of awareness surged between us, but then it disappeared, and I tried to pretend it never happened. "Oh, my God, what time is it?"

He glanced at his watch. "Ten."

"I gotta go." I wiped my mouth with a napkin and began gathering up the cartons to help clean up. "Thanks for dinner. I have to get home."

"I'll drive you."

"No, it's a short walk."

I clumsily tipped over the rice, and he grabbed my hand. "Quinn, you're not walking. I'll drive you home right now."

I held my breath, withdrew my hand, and nodded. "Okay. Thanks."

He dumped everything in the trash, grabbed his coat and keys, and headed out. The air was an arctic blast that numbed my skin, and I was glad for the ride. I shivered in my coat, and he clicked on the button to heat my seat. "Why did you move from Florida again?" I muttered, tucking my head down for warmth.

He laughed. "Too much sun makes you underappreciate a good day."

"Try me."

"Seriously, I missed the seasons. There's something about embracing the changes in the weather, like changes in life. When summer hits, I'll be able to savor every last drop of sunshine."

I smiled. "I like the way you think. You're a very positive person."

"So are you, Quinn Harmon."

The silence thickened. I swallowed, keeping my head down, and gave him the brief directions toward my apartment. Finally, he pulled up to the curb. "Thank you so much for the ride."

"Thanks for staying."

I slid off the seat, ready to jump out of the car, but he cut the engine and walked around to open my door. "Be careful. There's ice." Before I could say anything, he gripped my arm in a firm hold, tucking me into his body.

We reached the door, and I stepped quickly away. "Thanks again."

Very gently, he touched my cheek. "Any time."

Uncomfortable with the intimate look and his touch, I stepped back and fell into James's arms.

Oh, he was pissed.

A mixture of chilly displeasure and hot temper swirled in those blue eyes. "Hello, Brian," he clipped out. "I see we meet again."

Brian frowned. "I'm sorry I kept Quinn late at work."

James stared at him, his face tight. I knew he wanted to blast him, but knowing Brian was my boss, James managed to hold back. "Next time, let me know if she needs a ride. I can take care of her."

Tension swirled in the air. The challenge was delivered. Brian stepped back as if accepting defeat. "Of course. Good night."

James shut the door and dragged me inside. "What the hell is going on, Quinn?"

"I'm sorry! I know I texted you saying eight, but I had a patient intake, and it ran late, and then Brian ordered Chinese food, and we were talking, and I forgot about the time." My explanation sounded lame to my ears, but it was the truth. I took off my coat, turned, and saw the room.

Oh. My. God.

He'd set up a card table with a pretty floral tablecloth. Candles were lit, and the air was scented with apple spice. Two plates lay out with small portions of steak, baked potatoes, and green beans. A bottle of wine was uncorked in the center of the table. A white envelope lay on my chair. Stunned, I walked over to the beautiful table, my heart beating wildly. He'd set up the perfect dinner for me, and I'd ruined it. I squeezed my eyes shut, feeling like crap.

"James, I'm so sorry," I said again. "I didn't know you were going to do this."

"You're never late," he said. "When you say eight, you always mean eight. Why do you and Brian seem cozied up? What's really going on?"

"Nothing! He's just being nice to me, and it's all about work." A tiny sliver of guilt pierced through me, but I didn't want to say anything about a touch when it probably meant nothing. It would only make matters worse, and I couldn't have James upsetting my chance for the full-time job.

"You could've called me to pick you up."

"It was just faster! I swear, I didn't want this to happen. I was looking forward to seeing you tonight."

His face hardened. "But not enough, right?"

I went over to him and reached out, but he jerked back. Oh, boy, this was bad. I had to get him to understand. "James, I want this job. I thought you supported this."

"For God's sake, I've been supporting you endlessly! I want you to have it all, but lately, I feel like a fucking pity case, like I'm at the bottom of your list. We haven't talked or had a date or even fucked in a while. So, I'm asking again, what the hell is going on?"

My temper snapped. I was tired, stressed, and didn't need a jealous boyfriend making me feel guilty. "You're not a pity case. You're the man I love! Is it so hard to just be patient for a while? Everything is happening at once, and I just need some damn space!"

Silence fell between us. I bit my lip. That hadn't come out right. "I didn't mean—"

"Fuck this. You want space? I'll give you as much as you need. Let me know when you're available." He grabbed his jacket and headed toward the door.

"Don't leave! James, please. Aren't you staying over tonight?"

He shook his head and gave me a hard look. "You have a paper to write, remember? Call me when I'm not in the way."

The door slammed.

I fisted my hands. Tears burned my lids. What was happening to us? Why did I say such things when all I wanted was to be held in his arms? I went over to the table and opened up the envelope. The card was simple, a sketched-out caricature of a couple holding hands, sitting on a wall, watching a sunset. I opened it up and found the simple scrawl.

It's always been you, and always will be. Love, James.

I gripped the card tight between my fingers and vowed I'd fix everything.

Chapter Ten
James

I TRIED TO GET MY HEAD together when I walked into class. The whole scene with Quinn bothered me, and I hadn't slept at all last night. Finally, that morning, she'd called me. The moment I heard her voice, I forgave her. I knew we were both handling a lot, but seeing her come home, and that dickhead touching her cheek like he owned her, well, I just lost it. We both apologized and said we'd talk tomorrow night. I just had to work harder at finding more time to be with her. Especially in bed. Giving her multiple orgasms.

Ava was already speaking with one of the other students, so I set up my station. I loved the progress on my newest portrait, and felt solid she would, too. I'd followed the rules and incorporated all the techniques, but added another layer of whimsy I thought made it unique. The new sketch showed a woman after an orgasm, staring at her lover. I had worked hard on capturing that subtle gleam of polished skin after fucking; the softened, slightly bruised lips, the touch of wonderment and satisfaction in her eyes. I'd studied Quinn's face time and time again and would never get bored trying to capture the essence of her sexuality. It haunted me, pushing me to get it on paper.

Heels clicked and stopped behind me. The earthy scent of musk that reminded me of sex drifted to my nostrils. I felt Ava's scorching gaze take in my portrait, and my gut clenched. Ever since our conversation at the art store, I thought maybe she'd change her attitude toward me. Instead, she spent our last session treating me like shit, as if she'd never admitted I had raw talent.

I waited for a well-earned compliment, or something to tell me I wasn't wrong about thinking my portrait was damn good, but she never spoke, just moved on without another word.

Forget it. I'd never let her break me, or doubt myself with her games. I refused to give her that type of power.

"We're starting clean today," she announced. Her smart, red suit was a shock of brilliance in the gloomy, shadowed room. I guessed she'd run out of black this morning. No natural light shone through the windows today. It was just another dark, stormy day in Chicago. "I want you to use what we've been working on with the anatomy. Jason, will you come in here, please?"

A guy walked in. Young, clean-shaven head, dark eyes. He was tall, lean, with big feet and hands. He wore a white robe. He seemed not to give a crap that a roomful of art students were staring at him, and would not only paint but analyze every inch of his body over the next few days. He stood with a subtle arrogance and power I recognized. I'd never sketched a nude male before and promised myself I'd go for it, not allowing any societal barriers or embarrassment to block my creative energy.

"Class, this is Jason. You may take your position, please."

He shrugged off the robe. I got the impression of lean strength, a mass of dark, curly body hair, and a dick that would probably be pretty damn big if he was aroused. Thank God he wasn't. He lowered himself to the chair, stretching out his legs, propping his fist on his face in a pose resembling the Thinker, then stared out the window at something we couldn't see.

"I want to see a mingling of reality and intellectuality in this assignment. I want to own that look on his face, and at the same time feel as if I could reach out and touch the muscles on his body. Begin."

It took me a while to get out of my own head, but when I entered that free zone, I was off and flying. My fingers sketched until my muscles cramped, and the hours passed with just a few water breaks. I was on a kind of high as the afternoon wore on, until those red heels snapped their way to my station and a cold, mocking voice rose in the air.

"Are you afraid of a penis, Mr. Hunt?"

I stiffened. Low chuckles cut through the room. I gritted my teeth. "No."

"Good. And you have one, correct?"

More tittering. My ears turned red, but I did my best not to lose it. She was such a cold-hearted bitch. "Last I checked, I had one. I like it, too."

I cranked my head around to look her in the face. Show no fear. Her blood-red lips tightened, and she stared down at me with a haughty dignity I ached to ruffle. Why was she always on my shit? I had no idea what I ever did to her.

"Then I guess you rarely examined it, since the proportions seem oddly off-center."

One of the girls outright giggled, but I was locked in a staring match with the Ice Queen and refused to avert my gaze. "I disagree," I stated firmly. "If you'll look again, I think you'd find it's quite accurate."

Her nose crinkled, and her mouth pursed as if she'd tasted a lemon. She looked like I was a bug she craved to squash. I didn't back down, though. I had a feeling she ate men who didn't have the balls to stand up to her, and damned if I was going down when my life and career were at stake. She upped the ante.

"Perhaps you need a better view. Close up."

Silence fell. A strange tension lit the air between us, as if a game was being played where I didn't know the rules. I knew, in that moment, whatever I did would set the rest of the tone. I was sick to death of her exploiting my shit for the others and demeaning me on a daily basis.

I grinned. "Maybe you're right. I'll double-check." I pushed my chair out deliberately and strolled casually to the small, uplifted stage. Jason kept his pose, and I knelt down until my face was about even with his dick. Pretending to examine it while the class held their breath, I finally rose, slapped my hands together, and gave a thumbs-up signal.

"Nah, I'm good. I got it just about perfect."

The class burst into laughter. I grinned with them and swaggered back to my chair. Ava never moved, her delicate nostrils flared slightly like an angry mare. Her chilly green eyes gleamed with deadly intent.

"Thank you for the laugh, Mr. Hunt. Make sure you see me after class."

She clicked away. There were some low mutters among the class, but I pretended not to care, going back to my portrait. Inside, though, I was a mess, wondering if my pride had destroyed my opportunity to be in the show.

Finally, it was the end of the day, and most of the students had left. Jason had disappeared, and the class was empty. I packed up my shit, running my fingers over the lines of my portrait of the woman, thinking of Quinn. No reason to rush home, but maybe I'd get some sleep since I had the early shift at Joe's. I lingered, enjoying the silence and the smell of the art room, the peace of presence it gave me inside when I was surrounded by equipment I loved. I zipped up my art bag and heard a low moan.

My ears pricked. What the hell? I was supposed to meet with the Ice Queen, but I'd thought she'd left. Moving silently on my sneakers, I eased through the doorway and peeked my head around the corner into her battered office.

Another sound. Was she hurt?

I took one more step, ready to call out, and froze to my spot.

Ava was on her knees, facing me. Jason stood before her, naked, while she sucked his cock. As she worked him, his ass muscles tightened and he moved her head up and down, trying to control the pace, but I could already tell who was really in charge.

A sick fascination kept me rooted to the spot, along with total shock. What the hell was going on? I went to move back, to pretend I never saw the intimate scene, but her eyes snapped open, and she held my gaze like a boa constrictor squeezing me tight, refusing to allow me to move or even breathe.

Holy. Shit.

My teacher slid her tongue around his dick, her scarlet lips moving up and down with a suction that made Jason groan and mutter under his breath. He jerked his hips, but she never quickened her pace. Raw lust and a cold control shot from those green eyes, commanding me to watch her until she was done.

I meant to move. I tried to get my feet to lift from the ground and back away from this porno scene that was screwing with my head, but suddenly she grabbed his balls and began jerking her head hard, her lips closing tight, and then he was shouting and coming, and I was getting aroused by the sick show.

She swallowed, and when she raised her head and licked her lips, she gave me a small, triumphant smile.

Choking back a shocked cry, I finally got my body to listen and stumbled away from the door. My hands shook as I grabbed my art bag and flew out of the school.

What the hell was going on? That was some fucked-up power play, and I was in the middle of it without knowing why. Did she want to have sex with me? Torture me? Punish me?

I sensed that was no regular scene I just happened to interrupt. That was a well-rehearsed, well-constructed sex show meant just for my eyes. But why?

Before Quinn, I would've gotten off on the game. Hell, I'd lived for shit like that. Now? It just made me feel...dirty.

How the hell could I tell Quinn? The cold air hit my face hard and stole my breath, but it felt clean and pure. She knew I was having trouble with Ava, but after their meeting in the art store, there was no way I could explain that scene without it sounding like I'd done something with her. Especially since I didn't know Ava's intentions. Did Quinn really need to know? It wasn't like I did anything wrong. But I didn't like the idea that *not* telling her could be construed as a lie.

Shit.

I got back to my apartment and tried to stay distracted, but my whole body ached for Quinn. I needed to see her. Hold her close, remind myself of her goodness and natural sexiness that had nothing to do with games and manipulation. A reminder I didn't live in that world any longer. But she had class till late, and we'd planned to meet tomorrow to talk. I just had to deal with this on my own.

I had to talk to Ava. I refused to have a fucked-up teacher ruin everything. Maybe I'd try getting to class extra early so we could meet. Get to the bottom of her sick shit, and if I had to, I'd go to administration and complain. It was the only recourse that made sense.

Feeling calmer with a plan, I settled down for the night.

Chapter Eleven
Quinn

"QUINN, WE'RE GRABBING a drink. Come with us!"

I looked over from rolling up my yoga mat and shook my head. "I'm beat, guys."

The small group of four groaned, and Jessica stepped over, grabbing my mat from my fingers. "You said that last time. Girlfriend, take a break and have a damn drink with us!"

I laughed. In a matter of a few sessions, I'd grown close to the other four students enrolled in the special program at New Beginnings. They were a lot like me. Dedicated workaholics who wanted to make the world better. Each had their own personal addiction story—either themselves, or someone close—and we'd grown tight after a few sharing sessions.

Since our fight, James and I had talked on the phone, but we'd planned to get together tonight after his shift. Still, I had plenty of time for one drink. "Okay, but I can't stay long."

CHASING ME

Jessica whooped, putting away my mat, and I grabbed my coat and purse. "Hey, Brian, come on. You need a break, too!"

Brian's gaze swung around and rested on me. I shifted my feet. We hadn't mentioned the night he drove me home, and I was glad. He waved his hand in the air. "Go without me, young 'uns. I'm too old."

The group shouted good-natured insults. "You're like, what, dude? Thirty! Live a little."

After a bit of cajoling, Brian laughed. "Fine, fine, I'm coming."

We walked to the pub, and Jessica ordered us a round of beer. Sometimes I still got a craving for the fruity Sex on the Beach island drinks I'd gotten addicted to in Key West, but back in Chicago I reverted to wine again when I did drink. Wasn't much of a beer drinker, but I kept quiet since she was being nice.

We squeezed into a battered bar booth and raised our glasses. I couldn't resist the quip. "Hey, guys. Do you think it's a little weird we're working at a rehab and the first thing we want to do is get a cocktail?"

We shared a glance. Everyone seemed to ponder my question with good intention. Then Jessica spoke.

"Fuck no! Drink up!"

Everyone laughed. I sipped my beer, which still wasn't very good, and met Brian's eyes across the booth. His features took on a serious expression as he studied me, and I couldn't seem to look away. Jessica pulled the others away for a game of darts, and we were left alone at the table.

"Why didn't you tell her you hated beer?"

Startled at the question, I paused in my next sip. "How do you know?"

"Your face. It's expressive. You don't hide much."

"Doesn't matter. I don't drink much, anyway. Is that a good thing, or a bad thing?"

"Drinking?"

"No, showing how I feel."

"Good. Very good."

A warm hum sang between us. I cleared my throat and wished the others would come back. "I'm enjoying the extra classes."

He leaned back in the booth, holding his beer. "I can tell. You're extremely focused with your work."

I wrinkled my nose. "Yeah, my girlfriends are always trying to tell me to have more fun. People think I'm too serious."

"Does James agree?"

I flinched, dropped my gaze, and concentrated on my beer. "He helps me look at the world differently. Reminds me of things I usually forget."

Brian's voice went whisper-soft. "That's important. No one should go through life with limited vision. Yet something tells me you barely scratched the surface of who you really are, and what you'll do."

I sucked in my breath. The tension knotted tighter. It wasn't the same feeling I had when I was around James. No whipping, take-your-breath-away sexual chemistry. More like an awareness of who we were, and a familiarity I couldn't seem to wrap my head around. My mind screeched *Danger Zone*, even though we'd never touched and hadn't been inappropriate. But I felt guilty, and I couldn't figure out why.

I cleared my throat. "And you? Is work your world right now?"

"Yes. I graduated and got married right away."

I gasped, staring at him. "You're married?"

"Divorced." He slugged his beer then stretched his arms flat out on the table, his fingers a few inches from mine. His eyes held ghosts of the past. "We married too young. Didn't know who we were yet. A bunch of raw emotion and physical attraction does not make a future."

I squirmed in my seat. "What happened?"

"What happens to every young couple, mostly. We had different goals, work schedules conflicted, jealousy happened. We were torn apart. Got divorced two years later.

We're friends now, though. Both of us happier, and different people now." He paused. "James seemed angry when I took you home the other night."

Uneasy, I wasn't sure what to say. "We're fine now," I said.

"Good. My ex-wife and I had a volatile relationship."

I wondered why he seemed to be giving me some type of warning. The intensity built again, and suddenly he leaned forward, sliding his hand across the table, stopping a few inches from my own hand but not touching me. "You remind me so much of myself," he muttered. "Ambitious, bright, the world ahead of you. Be careful with your choices, Quinn. The world is your oyster. Don't limit yourself."

My mouth opened to respond, though I didn't know what I was going to say to him, but then everyone came back from the table and ordered nachos and began gossiping, and the moment passed.

I stayed another fifteen minutes, finished my beer, and said my goodbyes. Carefully avoiding Brian's gaze, I shot out the door and headed home, wondering what he was trying to tell me.

I was afraid, though, I already knew.

But it could have been my overactive imagination. Why would someone his age, with his position, be attracted to me? I wasn't even out of college, hadn't truly begun my career, and wasn't the flashy type to catch a man's eye. James always told me differently, but I was never too into my appearance. Sure, I liked surprising James with fancy underwear or cool shoes once in a while, and loved when he got that animal look in his eye that warned me he was about to fuck me hard and long, but Brian was a completely different type.

I was probably going nuts.

James was waiting for me when I got home. He looked up from the battered red couch and smiled. The television blared in the background—some reality show—and he rolled to his feet. Without a word, he closed the distance, took hold of my shoulders, and yanked me in tight.

My heart clutched, and I sank into his warmth, my arms clinging to him, his hard muscles cradling my softness. He just held me for a while, rubbing my back, burying his head in my hair, and in that moment, everything righted itself and was pure and good and right.

"I missed you," he whispered in my ear. I shivered and clung tighter.

"Me, too. I hate when we fight."

"So do I. Let's not do it again."

I laughed. My body lit up in its familiar way whenever I was in his presence, welcoming him to do any bad and dirty thing to me. But he didn't. Just kept me close, as if struggling with something. I opened my mouth to let him know I went to the bar for a drink after work, and Brian had been there, but figured it would only upset him. No need to bring it up when nothing happened. Only if he asked. "Are you okay?" I asked softly.

He paused. "Yeah. Long day."

"Is Ava still giving you a hard time?"

He stiffened and pulled away. Not meeting my gaze, he took my hand and pulled me to the couch. I fell onto his lap and snuggled in. "I can handle it. I'm almost ready to show you my new portrait. I'm excited about it."

I pushed back his thick hair and peered at his face. I'd changed my mind about Ava, figuring she was one of those teachers who tortured the students who were really good, but his frustration was evident. I knew exactly how it felt to have a professor give me a hard time, and my endless goal to finally get her to like me. Having your entire career judged by one person was hard, especially when James already struggled with his confidence in his abilities. Probably best to not question him further and let him work it out.

I stroked his muscular chest. He smelled like clean cotton, and his soft T-shirt stretched over strong shoulders, making me feel protected and safe. When I looked at his art,

I felt like he left a piece of himself behind, hidden. I adored being around such talent, because I had none of that stuff. As a Virgo, I was earthly, solid, dependable, boring. Not James. He was bigger and brighter, and made me want to savor every part of his magic. I tried to tell him that many times, but he laughed it off, saying I was the one who made him a better man. I hoped he kept believing it.

"You'll be picked for the show," I said confidently.

"Sounds like a fairy tale where everything works out in the end."

"Don't you believe in happily ever after?" I teased. "I saw you sneaking a peek at my Kindle last week. You like romance."

"I like the sex parts," he corrected.

I tickled him under the ribs, his one sensitive spot, and he growled and wrestled me to the couch. I kicked and screamed helplessly as he tortured all my sensitive body parts, until my cries for mercy were finally heeded.

"James?"

"Yeah?"

I gazed up into his beautiful aquamarine eyes, cupping his cheeks, and knew we were meant to be together, no matter how many obstacles got in our way. "You're my happily ever after."

His face softened, and he kissed me long and sweet for endless moments. I fell into bliss and that wonderful bubble of emotion and need that lit me up and satisfied the hole in my soul.

"You're gonna get a few orgasms for that remark."

I laughed as he picked me up and carried me into the bedroom.

I pushed all thoughts of Brian and Ava out of my mind and concentrated on the man I loved, and our happily ever after.

Chapter Twelve
James

I ARRIVED EARLY AT the Brush Institute. It had been over a week since Ava's porno show, and she seemed to have backed off. I'd planned to confront her after seeing her with Jason, but she hadn't been in for a few days, and then readily ignored me. By that time, I tried to convince myself shit like that wouldn't happen again.

I hoped to God I was right.

I set up my canvas and charcoals, chatted with one of the other students, and tried to get my head back in the game. Today was the day we showed our final sketches, and Ava would make a decision on who to pick for the expo. Only five were chosen from the whole school, and with over one hundred students taking various classes, slots were tight.

The exhibition was advertised by the art museum and local shops in the area and brought out a huge crowd, along with interested patrons, buyers, and art dealers. Basically, it was exposure that was pretty much priceless.

If I had wanted to use my parents' connections, I could probably make a few calls and get someone to take a look, but I wanted this on my own. Wanted it so badly I woke up in the middle of the night, craving the opportunity like I'd used to crave getting off with a girl as a teen. Was this what it was like to be part of the everyday crowd? No special deals to be made, or palms to be greased, or bargains to be made? Just you and your talent up against everyone else's?

I wasn't stupid. I still knew politics were important. But this was the first time I was fighting for something on my own, and it felt good, like I was coming into myself. I wanted to prove to myself and Quinn I was worth the risk.

Ava walked in. She was back to her usual black and wore silk pants, a low-cut blouse, and jacket. Her red hair was twisted in a severe chignon, emphasizing her pale skin and ruby lips. She looked...cold. Formidable. Ready to tear down whoever was blocking the empty road in front of her.

She began speaking immediately, going over the rules of the exhibit and asking everyone to turn in their final projects.

I worked nonstop for the next few hours, skipped lunch break, and finished up. I had a late night shift at Joe's, and hoped to swing by the center to see Quinn before her extra class started.

One by one, the students went to see Ava in her office with their project. We were all nervous as shit, but trying to pretend we didn't care. She called me last, which was fitting, because I didn't want an audience when I came back out.

I brought in my portrait of the woman, along with the sketch of naked Jason from my portfolio, which I actually really liked. Ava was sitting behind the desk, clicking away at her computer, ignoring me. I gritted my teeth, took a seat across from her, and waited.

"Give me your final project, please."

I handed it over. She didn't even glance at it, just put it in a toppling pile behind her with canvases, drawings, and one sculpture. Finally, she faced me, crossing her legs and leaning back slightly in her chair. Her face was devoid of emotion.

"You think you're hot shit, don't you, Mr. Hunt?"

Oh, yeah, that was it. I'd officially had enough and was gonna tell it like it was. She was going to do whatever the hell she wanted anyway, regardless of my mouth. "Not really. But you do."

A smile touched her red lips. "The moment you walked into my class, you thought you were better than anyone else. Fought me on structure, basic ground rules, and techniques, saying you were ahead of the rest, though you had no formal training. Am I correct?"

I refused to squirm in my seat. Yeah, I'd been pissed to start off at an introductory class, but now admitted I had needed it. I shrugged. "You proved your point."

"I know who you are. Who your parents are. That you're a trust-fund baby. Why not make it easy on yourself? Make a phone call and get your own showing. You don't need ours."

I watched my dream slip away because of a bitch with a need to show me my place. "You know nothing about me," I ground out. "I don't know what sick mind games you're playing, but you're not dragging me into them. I'm going to administration. Maybe you can suck the Dean's dick, in addition to your male model's."

I went to get up, but her voice cut like a whiplash. "Sit down, Mr. Hunt. I'm not done with you."

"What did I ever do to you? I just want to fucking learn and have a fair shot at the exhibition."

"Because I don't want to waste my time," she shot back. "When I take on an artist, I go full throttle, and I don't want someone who's playing around to kill some time before he goes back to his trust-fund money."

Un-fucking believable. I gazed at her in astonishment. "Who are you, anyway? I don't need you to mentor me. I need you to judge my work fairly and give a recommendation!"

"You don't get it, do you?" she asked. Her red nail tapped the blotter on her desk. "This exhibition is the beginning of a whole new world. The last three years, the students I personally chose hit the big time. Private showings. Art dealers begging for their work and artists setting their own price. I mentored every single one of them, bled on their behalf, and pushed them beyond their limits. I pick one student to mentor, Mr. Hunt, and that's the only one who ever succeeds."

Her ego was massive. I stared at her, trying to get my brain to click back on and understand what I was dealing with. "I don't need your help or your private mentorship," I shot back. "Did you do this with the others? What kind of school is this?"

"No, I didn't do this with the others. You're an extreme case. You can go ahead and let the Dean know. I'll admit to having an affair with my male model and that you walked in on us by accident. I'll tell him I pushed you, was rude, and called you out in class. We can conference, and you can go through channels, but it's not like I'm blackmailing you with sex or favors to get ahead."

"What the hell was that shit with Jason? What are you trying to prove? You looked at me. You planned for me to walk in and catch you."

Her gaze locked on mine. She leaned forward and lowered her voice to a husky growl. "You have passion in your work. More than passion. It's a raw, rough quality that grabs an onlooker and makes you stop to look deeper. You can't teach that. But it was too undirected and unformed, and that quality wasn't in every one of your sketches. Only a few. I figured it could be a fluke, so I conducted an experiment."

I felt like I was being led deeper into Wonderland, and it was a drug bust instead of a happy retreat. "What experiment?"

"Your girlfriend was quite interesting, Mr. Hunt?"

Red misted my vision. My hands clenched. "My girlfriend has nothing to do with you and your crazy-ass games."

"You love her?"

"Yes."

"Well, that love is killing your muse."

I blinked. What the fuck? I laughed humorlessly, shaking my head. "You're crazy."

"Every time I pushed your buttons, you delved deeper. Darker. When I let you slide, and you went back to your comfortable life, that's what you gave me. Comfort. People don't want comfort. They want to feel things, mostly awful, dark, secret things."

She reached out and grabbed the portrait of Jason from my hands. Jabbing a finger at it, she turned it to me. "See this? Look at his expression. The lines of his body. There's something almost sexual, and wrong, and shameful about this pose. Not one of the other students gave it to me—they just sketched a good-looking naked guy staring into space. You used the emotions you saw the other day when you caught me with Jason, dug deep, and gave me something different."

I stared at the sketch I was so proud of. And saw it. The sexual gleam in his eye, the way he tilted his jaw, the slight thrust of his hips, as if imagining something he never wanted to delve into. The tiny facets of light and shadow and meaning exploded forth, and in that moment, I got it. Got what she was saying, though it was crazy, and impossible, and a road not to be followed. I thought back to those raging emotions when I watched Ava sucking him off, and realized I'd translated it back to the page.

My hands shook. "That's not true. Just coincidence. You're looking for an excuse to keep playing your mind fuck."

Her smile was flawless as she threw the portrait down. "You like a good mind fuck, Mr. Hunt. It's what you were built on. Trying to change it by settling down with a good girl and working at a coffee shop, fading into the woodwork, is eventually going to destroy you."

"I love Quinn. She saved me. Don't you get it? I was numb before her."

She studied me thoughtfully. "You believe it, don't you? That love can save you? Make you better? You don't need saving. You need to hone your talent so you can have a lifelong career pursuing art. You need to get down and dirty and be truthful with yourself. But you need to make a choice."

"My career or my girlfriend? There is no choice. I'd pick Quinn every time. But I don't believe in that shit. I don't need to make a choice. I can have both."

"Not if she doesn't allow you to tap into that wild part of you. The untamed, inner you that makes no sense. Because that is what drives great art."

"She does."

"I met her, Mr. Hunt. Girls like her don't inspire that type of ugliness. I don't believe you. And if you don't take this seriously, I'm not interested in going further. If I took you on, we'd be spending a large amount of time together. I wouldn't let you be afraid of being who you are. In fact, I'd demand it. Push you." Her gaze turned sexual, flicking over my body in a way that made me want to squirm. "And I bet you'd like it."

I burned from the inside until I wanted to rage, throw things, howl. I breathed deep, trying to get calm, while she smirked. "So, you're saying unless I dump my girlfriend, you won't put me in the expo?" I finally asked.

"I said no such thing. I just told you to get your priorities in order and make sure you can deliver. Some of us aren't meant to be civilized or contained, Mr. Hunt. The sooner you realize that, the better you'll be. You're dismissed."

I leapt to my feet. "I don't need your threats, or your fucking expo, or your school."

"Very well, then. Good luck."

I slammed the door, cursing nonstop, feeling the wild rage pour out of me in choppy waves, ready to drown me alive. My whole body shook, and I headed out into the streets, walking and trying to clear my mind.

It was over.

There'd be no show. *Who gives a shit?* I thought. I didn't need the Brush Institute. I'd enlist somewhere else, or find a mentor, or study by myself. It had been working before. I'd heard of these hard luck stories of artists getting discovered and making it big, of never quitting and finally achieving success.

But where? the inner voice taunted. Joe's Cafe, smelling of sweat and coffee? The corner of Millennium Park, painting passersby? The art department in some office building?

I'd find a way. I had Quinn and a strong mind, and I was capable. I just needed to sit down and think of my options, then make a new plan.

My phone shrieked. I grabbed it, assuming it was Quinn, and spoke into the receiver. "I'm on my way to the clinic to see you."

"James? Where are you? What are you talking about?"

I stopped mid-flight, squeezing my eyes shut. Well, wasn't this shit day getting worse. My mother's voice held a tinge of worry, but I knew already it wasn't for my welfare. Oh, no, she'd heard the gossip, and called personally to make sure her only son didn't humiliate the family name.

"Mom. Sorry, I thought you were someone else. What do you want?"

"You never returned my last two phone calls. Your father was angry, but I explained you were probably quite busy and planned to get back to us soon. Are you very busy?"

Her barbed intent hit home. Funny, I didn't remember many soft times between us, the way a mother and son were supposed to be. At least from what I saw in the movies or witnessed with other guys. She never fussed over me or babied me. The nannies raised me, gave little comfort, and I spent most of my time trying to catch my father's attention. My mother had already checked out, making sure I was bathed and dressed and polite at all functions. Making sure I fit the ideal image of what she wanted me to be, but she rarely delved deep enough to seek out who I was. I mourned, rebelled, and did all the normal things, but then I just detached. She made it kind of easy. She was never mean, or cruel, just distant. After a while, it seemed like I was fighting for...nothing.

"Yes, I'm busy."

"Serving coffee for our friends' children in Chicago?"

Displeasure rattled her voice. "I'm putting myself through art school. I told you last year, Mother, I intend to make it on my own. I'm not touching my trust fund. I left Key West, sold the yacht, my bike, and all my other stuff. Isn't that what you always wanted for me? To be independent and honorable?"

I made sure to sweeten my voice, forcing her to play her hand. "Honorable, yes. But not at this expense. James, we gave you that trust fund for your future. We expected you to use it to find a career and make a man out of yourself, not to make a mockery of your family. Do you realize the position you put us in? All of your father's friends called to find out why you're working at a coffee shop. He was humiliated and forced to make up a story. Why would you do this to us, James?"

I should've have been upset or disappointed. Not after the past. I knew better. But damned if every time I spoke with my mother or father I didn't pray something would change. I realized then, for the final time, nothing ever would. I could become a hot-shit artist, well known around the world, and still my parents wouldn't approve or be satisfied. Maybe if I'd gone into business, or done medicine or law. Maybe. But even then, they wouldn't have cared if I were happy.

I stood in the middle of the busy street, in the cold, with the phone pressed to my ear. A flood of raw emotion made my whole body shake, but there was nothing to do but stand up for myself.

No one else would.

I took a deep breath. Normally, I'd bitch and rage at my parents in a frustrated attempt to get them to listen. But today, I spoke calmly. "Mother, I'm sorry you don't approve. But I'm not taking that money, at least, not any longer. The work sucks, but it's honest, and it helps pay the rent. Just tell Dad's friends I'm experimenting with being a starving artist."

There was a long pause. I felt her thinking of how to fix the situation to make it palatable. Finally, she spoke. "Come home, James. We'll start over. Find you something you'll be happy with, maybe find a girl you can settle down with. It's not too late."

My heart twanged. Come home. How many times did I wish and pray for them to want me to come home? But this was for their own benefit, so they could control me. My throat tightened. "No, Mother, I can't. I'm already in love with someone. Her name is Quinn, and that's why I'm in Chicago. She's amazing."

"Another so-called artist?" my mother asked snobbily.

I let out a breath. "No, a social worker. She's way too good for us."

My mother's sharp gasp made me smile. "We can't let this happen, James. Please don't force us to interfere. If you must pursue art, at least use your money to set up a gallery or something respectable."

God, it would be so damn easy. Open up my own business, display my art, get investors. But my success wouldn't be valid, and I needed to finally do something on my own. Something important.

My voice hardened. "I'd advise you to keep doing what you've always done, Mother. Ignore me. Let me live my life on my own. We've been perfecting it for over twenty years now, right?"

"James Hunt! You will listen to me, or you'll be talking with your father."

"Thanks for checking on me. Goodbye." I clicked off as gently as possible, already knowing the shit had hit the fan. Dad would be next, but I'd screen. Eventually, the gossip would die down, and they'd get distracted with something else until I faded from their minds again.

I hurried my pace, desperate to see Quinn.

Chapter Thirteen
Quinn

I CHECKED MY PHONE, hoping to have heard from James, but no one had texted. I knew today he'd handed in his portrait for consideration in the show. I thought of that awful teacher giving him a hard time after all his work, and wanted to punch her in the face.

Very unlike me.

I was so tired. The additional classes at New Beginnings were great, but between the heavy workload for the Spring semester and my two jobs, I was exhausted all the time. Still, if I could only push till May, everything would fall into place. I'd graduate, get a full-time job, quit my volunteer position at the nursing home, and concentrate on building a life. With James. My master's degree could wait for a while, or maybe I could do it part-time and take it slow.

"Quinn?" Brian stepped out of his office. "Can I see you for a moment?"

My heart pounded. I hoped I hadn't done anything wrong. The trial classes were almost finished, and I'd bonded with the other students, hating that we seemed to be competing for one available position. Still, we were very alike, and I had a feeling we'd stay close no matter who was chosen for the job. I tried to act professional and cool as I walked into his office and took a seat in the chair.

Brian didn't sit behind the desk. Instead, he took a seat on the side, closer to me, hooking one ankle over his knee in a casual gesture that bespoke a confident, professional male.

"I've made a decision about the full-time position," he said.

I held my breath.

"I want to offer it to you."

I exhaled in a long whoosh, feeling a bit giddy and unstable even seated. A warm smile curved his lips at my obvious joy, though I tried to act cool and pretend I had always believed I'd get the job.

"Thank you, Brian. I know it was a hard decision, but I promise you won't regret your decision."

He nodded, scanning my face, his gaze probing mine. That weird jump in my stomach happened again, but I ignored it. "I know I won't, Quinn. Believe me, I've been watching everyone carefully through these classes. I was going to wait to make my decision in May, when the opening occurs, but I didn't want you to wonder or stress during finals. You've worked hard. You earned it. It's not going to be easy. Unfortunately, with most of these types of jobs, the hours are too long and the pay isn't great. Double shifts are common. I'll need you to cover odd weekends and nights, and your schedule won't be structured for a while. You'll be put through the paces, but I believe in you and what you can do for this clinic."

I blinked away the ridiculous sting of tears. It had finally happened. All my hard work had been worth it, and the only thing I wanted to do was run through the streets and tell James. I wanted to celebrate with him, to feel his mouth on mine. See his smile and hear him tell me he always knew I could do it.

"Thank you," I said again.

He grinned, got up from the seat, and handed me a thick folder. "This is all the paperwork regarding the job. It details pay, bonuses, benefits, and vacation policies. I'm going to ask you to keep it under wraps until I can personally speak with the others."

"Of course." I took the file, and we stood a bit awkwardly, looking at one another. Finally, he leaned over and gave me a quick, hard hug. "Congratulations, Quinn Harmon," he murmured in my ear. "I see great things for you."

I hugged him back, but there was a warm, friendly vibe that wrapped around me, and I realized as similar as we were, we didn't have the spark I had with James. I pulled back, gave him another thank-you, and rushed out the door.

Quickly, I pulled out my phone and texted James. *Have news. On my way to your place.*

I ran all the way, but when I got to his apartment, he wasn't there. Fishing my key out of my purse, I let myself in to wait for him. Tonight would be perfect. Maybe we'd splurge on dinner. He was done with his art project and would get into the expo, and I got my full-time job. We'd finally have some money and a solid future.

Feeling like I was ready to bust, I quickly called my dad and left him a voicemail, telling him I had great news. Then I decided to call my girls. Honestly, nothing good or bad happened in my life without my BFFs being involved.

Crossing my fingers they'd both be available, I brought up Skype and tried Cassie first. Her face popped up on my screen. "I'm here."

"Cassie, I miss you!"

Cassie sighed and gave me a weak smile. "I know, sweetie. I miss you too. It's been crazy here making sure I get my straight A's and dealing with some stuff."

"Stuff?" I asked. "Does this have to do with Ty?"

Her face plainly reflected pain that hadn't faded yet. "No, he hasn't contacted me. I have to testify at the trial in Key West soon, and I'm nervous."

"I know. But you need to do this, and it's going to be okay. Mac and I will arrive a few days afterward and make sure you're okay. I wish I could get out there earlier to help, but it was hard just taking a few days off at work."

"No, I totally understand. How is the clinic?"

I grinned widely. "I have news. Can we get Mac on?"

"Hell, yes. She knows to pick up from us unless she's onstage."

I laughed, dialed her in, and sure enough, my second best friend was reflected on the screen. "Hey, girls. What's shakin?" Her country twang and gorgeous face made me miss her even more.

"Two things. One, we want to be sure you're okay. The last time we spoke, you broke up with Austin."

The sadness in her eyes tore my heart apart. Answer given. I guessed she and Austin weren't doing too well. "I'm hanging in. Throwing myself into work, you know? Maybe I'll get another top country hit due to my broken heart."

I jumped in. "I'm sorry, sweetie. We'll be there soon. Can you hang in?"

Mac smiled. "Absolutely! I'm keeping busy trying to clear my schedule so we can spend some quality time together. What's the second thing you called for?"

I knew she meant it, so I accepted her answer. Cassie's small nod said she did, too. "I have good news."

Mac grinned. "Good, we need it. Tell all."

"I got the full-time position at New Beginnings!"

They both squealed and clapped and made a big deal out of it. Mac thought I needed more fun in my life, and Cassie was always telling me to try to have balance, but they knew how hard I'd worked for this.

"I can't wait to celebrate!" Mac announced. "Congratulations, darlin'. You so deserve it."

"I never doubted you," Cassie swore. "Do you start after graduation?"

"Yes, I already put in for vacation for Spring Break, so that's still clear."

"I bet James is just as excited," Cassie mentioned.

"I'm waiting to tell him. Figured I'd call my girls first."

"You better!" Mac warned. "Forget that 'bros before hoes' crap. It's BFFs before boyfriends!"

We all laughed, chattered a bit, then finally ended the call.

I dropped onto the couch, checking to see if he'd texted back yet, and tried to enjoy the few moments of happiness and satisfaction. I was hard on myself, so I figured after a few days, I'd be on to the next goal to conquer.

But for now, in this moment, life was just about perfect.

Chapter Fourteen

James

I SWITCHED MY CELL TO SILENT to ward off a call from my dad, and asked the receptionist if Quinn was still around. "Oh, she was just in Brian's office. Let me ring and see if she's still there."

I stiffened at the sound of Brian's name, but swore I'd be an adult. There was no reason to believe anything else was going on, even if Brian was interested. Quinn just wasn't that type of woman.

The receptionist—her name tag said Sharon—clicked off the phone and motioned upstairs. "Take the elevator to the second floor. First door on the left."

"Great, thanks." I headed up, then knocked. Brian opened the door. "Hey, Brian. Don't mean to interrupt. I was looking for Quinn."

Oh, yeah. This guy was not a fan of mine. A grim smile touched his lips, but he seemed to try to be friendly. "No problem. She left."

"Oh, sorry. Thanks." I turned, but he called out my name. "Yeah?"

"I'd like to talk to you for a second. Do you have time?"

This time, our gazes met and clashed. "Sure." I walked in, assessing his neat and orderly office, complete with a row of impressive degrees, all framed and hung on the wall behind his desk. Trophies from sports lined his bookcases. Yep, an overachiever. Even his office smelled faintly of lemon polish, as if he dusted it every day.

He's a lot like Quinn, the voice whispered inside me.

I ignored the voice and took a seat. The worn leather creaked gently under my weight. Brian straightened out his desk, then steepled his fingers and spoke. "Quinn is doing quite well here. I don't want to spoil her news in case she wanted to surprise you, so I hope you don't say anything. I offered her a full-time position at the center."

Joy and pride rushed through me. I grinned, so damn happy for her. She'd been busting her ass for years, and it finally paid off. I shook my head, trying to keep my emotions in check. "That's great news. Nah, I won't let her know I got tipped off. You made the right choice. Quinn won't let you down."

"I'm not worried about Quinn," Brian said firmly. "I'm more worried about her relationship with you."

And just like that, the boxing gloves were thrown into the ring.

I grabbed them right away. "Do you think I'm stupid?" I asked softly. "I know you're into her. I know you've been whispering in her ear, probably talking shit about me. But if you think you can tempt Quinn away, you don't know her at all. She loves me."

His lips thinned. "We've talked a lot over the past few weeks. Yes, she loves you. But I also know you're holding her back. I know she's already wracked with guilt, trying to meet her responsibilities yet keep you happy. How many times has she apologized for the late nights and extra workloads? You think her schedule will get better? It won't. I push my full-timers to complete their master's degree and go through additional training. You're uneducated. Working at a coffee shop. Yes, you're a serious artist, which I commend. But how long before you can support yourself? Is Quinn going to support you while you try your hand at making it in a competitive world where the percentages are against you?"

"You're an asshole." I fumed, swallowing past my desire to beat the shit out of him. "I know how guys like you work. You play the mentor role with her, put a few bugs in her ear that she deserves better, and then step in when things get rough. I bet you want me to rush home and tell her about this conversation. You'd like that, wouldn't you? You could play the wounded boss, deny it, say I misconstrued and I'm a hot-tempered little boy. But Quinn is worth more than that to me. I would never put her job at risk for a piece of shit like you."

I got up from the chair, too disgusted to continue. I'd have to figure out how to move forward without telling Quinn, but damned if I'd ruin her good news or her satisfaction in finally reaching her goals. She deserved more.

More than you, the voice said. *Brian may be right. You have nothing to offer her.*

Of course, I had a million dollars in my trust fund, just ready to use. But I knew if I dipped into my parents' money, I'd sell myself out for good. There'd be no going back or carving my own way. I'd be successful and keep Quinn. But inside, I'd be a lie, and it would eat a piece of my soul every day of my life until I was nothing but a shell.

"You don't understand, James. I'm not trying to outwit you for the girl. I'm telling you this because I know, man. I was there. I got married to a girl when we were young, and we tore each other apart. Quinn needs stability. She's her own worst enemy because she's driven to succeed at everything she does. It's the classic trait of the child of an alcoholic. She'll race far ahead of you in her drive to help others and be the best, and the guilt will cripple her when you can't keep up. I don't want to see you both destroyed." Brian paused, and his face changed from that of a man trying to beat a competitor to more of a confidant. His voice came out a bit husky. "You're going to break her heart without even knowing it."

Everything inside me stilled. Rebelled and screamed against the words that peppered my soul like bullets. Wanting to howl with the pain, I managed to keep my shit together and not show him how his speech affected me.

"If you care about Quinn at all, keep your distance. And leave us alone."

I left. Walked for a while. Checked my phone and got Quinn's text about waiting for me at home. My head hurt like I had a morning hangover.

Was I wrong? Everyone kept telling me the same thing over and over. My friends. My parents. My art teacher. Brian. I wasn't good for Quinn. We were too different, and I'd never be who she needed. I'd never be able to make her happy.

Had she been confiding in Brian about our relationship this whole time? Were their heart-to-hearts becoming more, but she was afraid to tell me?

I walked, and thought, while it darkened and the full moon peeked out to play with the grumpy night clouds. I didn't know what to do. If I were strong enough, maybe I'd sacrifice my own happiness and let her go, but the thought made my every iota buck in sheer denial. No way was I giving up Quinn. I'd find a way to give her what she wanted if it killed me.

I finally went home, took the long, deep breath yogis always talked about, and walked in.

"Finally!" She jumped up from the couch, a gorgeous sparkle in those inky eyes, and launched herself at me. I caught her, held her close, and wondered why I suddenly had a sick pit in my stomach. *Focus. I needed to focus.*

"I texted you, and I was waiting, and I wanted to tell you all calm, and maybe plan it, but I can't wait, I have to tell you now! I got the job, James! I got the full-time job at the New Beginnings! Brian told me today."

I grabbed her tight, loving the flush on her cheeks and the curve of her soft lips, and damned if I didn't almost choke up, I was so fucking happy for her. Sometimes, in Quinn's presence, I felt like I was around greatness. Not the sugary, clichéd type of do-gooders I'd heard of before. No, Quinn just vibrated at a higher level, all intensity and purity, every part of her soul making mine lighter and more whole.

"I'm so proud of you, baby," I murmured in her ear. "Not surprised. Just proud."

She laughed, clinging to me, then gripped the back of my head and brought it down, feasting on my mouth like she was ravenous, and I was a perfectly cooked rib eye, ready to eat. She gave me everything in that kiss, her lips opening wide, arching up so her sweet breasts cushioned my chest, and I had no doubt she was aroused and ready to go. I grew hard and thick, my jeans shrinking in a matter of seconds, and I wanted her so fucking bad, craved to rip off her pants, part her legs, shove her over the couch, and pound inside of her, over and over, so deep and hard she'd never think of another man again.

I took the kiss deeper, rougher, and she ate it up, practically burning up in my arms for me, my touch, my cock, and something exploded within me. I tore off her sweater, panting hard, and she ripped at my jeans, shoving down my underwear and stroking my cock, until I almost lost it and precum coated the tip, and I was crazed to take her.

"Yes, now, now," she chanted, dropping to the floor and pulling me down on top of her. I growled, shoved her panties aside, and got ready to plunge deep, like the animal everyone believed I was, the animal I *knew* I was.

I hesitated one moment. Looked at her face. And almost broke apart.

Her eyes were closed, lips parted, gasping for breath as she waited for me to fuck her. I remembered that first day on my yacht in Key West when I took her for the first time. She surprised me with her wildness and innate sexuality, allowing me to go deep into my hidden fantasies and claim her the way I craved. In passion, in anger, in celebration, in frustration. The dark, seething intensity inside me sprang free, but it scared the shit out of me, who I really was. I wanted to fuck her with everything uncivilized, until there was nothing left of either of us.

Dear God, Quinn deserved more. She should have been demanding care and tenderness. She should have been made love to like a fucking goddess I worshipped, not like this, on the dirty floor, with her underwear shoved aside like a whore.

I cringed, but it was too late for me. Already, I was losing control, ready to come just from the musky scent of her arousal, inches from her sweet pussy I wanted to claim. I clenched my teeth, shut my eyes, and scrambled for control. Then I slid home.

She fisted me so tight and hot, rocking her hips and moaning for more, always more. Knowing what she needed to get off, I refused to use her hard like I wanted to, and kept my strokes long and even, bringing her higher in a controlled way, making sure to hit the spot she liked, my thumb resting gently on her clit and rubbing in small circles.

She cried out my name, twisting for more, and her drugged eyes locked with mine in an effort to get me to go faster, harder, to lose control completely. I thrust in and out, refusing to screw her without care, and took her at a slow, steady pace. I pressed my thumb harder against her clit, finally quickening my pace, and I felt her coming, shattering around my dick. I drank in every expression on her face, knowing I gave her this, the release she needed so much, and then I couldn't think anymore because I was coming hard and long, my guttural wail ripping from my lips.

I'm not sure how long we lay together, tangled on the worn, cheap carpet. Her voice drifted in the air.

"Why are you holding back?"

I lifted my head. A tiny frown creased her brow, and her brown eyes held a light of worry. "What do you mean? If that was holding back, I'm definitely not doing my job."

She laughed, but it didn't reach her eyes. Instead, she lowered her gaze and shifted. "I mean, I just noticed you seem to treat me a little, umm, differently. Like, softer, you know?"

I caught her blush and knew she was uncomfortable talking about it. Had she noticed I was trying harder? Women liked men who made love. I wanted to worship her in every way possible, and damned if I couldn't take it to the bedroom. Like Brian would, if she ever belonged to him. Which she never would. "You deserve sweetness, baby." I stroked her hair back from her face with gentle motions. "You deserve to be treated like a fucking queen."

Her lips curved in a smile, and I leaned in, pressing a kiss to her neck. "Don't be afraid I'll break, James," she said. "I want to give you...everything."

My heart splintered, and I rolled her on top of me, kissing her swollen, sweet mouth. "You already do. I won't let you forget it, Quinn. Ever."

She gasped, as if suddenly realizing something important. "Oh, my God, James, I'm sorry. I forgot to ask you about your portrait. Did you hand it in?"

I kept my face impassive. "Yeah."

"And? Did Ava love it?"

My mind went over the crazy-ass scene at the Brush Institute, and Ava's insistence I leave Quinn in order to protect my art. I tried to pick my words carefully. "I don't think I got it, baby. I may need to look at some other options."

She turned around and grabbed my face. Her dark eyes shot sparks of fire. "We're going to fight the decision. You deserve it! You need to talk to Ava."

My stomach twisted. I had to tell her the truth. But not tonight. Not now. "It was a long shot. I'm not going to let it stop me. I'm checking into some other art schools. Maybe I'll try to get a position in an art museum. Something. Anything."

She huffed out a breath. "I'm so mad! I know you're the best. James, I feel things when I look at your drawings I've never felt before. And it has nothing to do with being in love with you. You need to fight it."

"I will. Let me wait until final selections are made Wednesday. I just don't want you to worry if I don't make it. I'll work something out." I kept my voice firm and steady, wanting her to believe I could take care of my own shit so she didn't always have to worry if I was a step behind her.

You'll bring her down. You'll break her heart.

Fuck you.

"I'm not worried, I'm pissed. There's a difference." She looked so damn cute with the pout on her lips and fire in her eyes, I had to laugh.

"Come on, Rocky Balboa. Let's go celebrate with some deep-dish."

"James, are you ready to leave for Key West next week?" she asked. "I mean, I know we bought the tickets already, but if you feel like you need to stay to work things out, I'll stay with you."

I knew she would. But Quinn needed to be with her friends and relax before she started a new chapter in her life. I wanted that time with her, away from the daily stresses, and didn't care what happened. I was going.

"No way are we staying home," I said firmly, tugging on my clothes. "I can't wait to see you in that red bikini. We're all set, and there's no reason to cancel."

Her brow smoothed out, and I knew I'd make it happen. No matter what it took.

Chapter Fifteen
Quinn

I CRAMMED INTO A booth with the rest of my crew to celebrate our last day of classes at New Beginnings. Everyone was hopeful but supportive of one another, and I tried very hard not to give anything away, feeling a twinge of guilt at being picked. Brian didn't let on he'd made a decision, and he ordered a round of appetizers for the table, toasting to his incredible team and what we all brought to the residents.

I'd told my dad a few nights ago, and the gruffness of his voice told me how proud he was. It felt so good, finally getting what I wanted for so long. I just hated that James didn't get what he deserved.

My mind wandered as the table broke into a variety of gossip and general chatter. There was a strange ache in my gut that told me something was wrong. I couldn't pinpoint it, and had even tried to ignore it, but James seemed off. It wasn't about an outright lie. I thought I'd spot that immediately. It was more a general sense of discontent.

Cassie would quote Shakespeare at this point, which would make me laugh. I wished I could go see her and talk it out, but she was in Key West testifying in the trial. I wouldn't bug her with my psychic babblings of things about to go wrong.

But I did feel it. Something was about to go wrong.

I let out an annoyed breath and wondered if I'd ever be able to kick back and relax for longer than a day. I was always scurrying back to the rat race, or anticipating doom and gloom. Still, I was usually right.

James had changed. He held a secret, or a thought he didn't want to share with me. I felt it the most during sex. His usual ferocity in the bedroom, that gorgeous, rough, raw quality that reminded me of a sleek animal in the wild, was tamed. It was almost as if he was afraid to let go with me, no matter how hard I urged him to. His lovemaking was controlled and tender, but was missing an element that had burned between us from the moment we met.

Was he getting bored of me?

I shifted in the booth uneasily and sucked at my Coke, having adeptly maneuvered out of drinking beer tonight. When I tried to bring it up before, he'd told me he always wanted me. His words still rang true. His gaze still seethed with a fiery lust I adored. But when he touched me, he was careful, refusing to take me in the ways I dreamed of.

"Quinn? Are you okay?"

I looked up. Brian was staring at me with a hard intensity that made me a bit uncomfortable. I hoped he wasn't getting the wrong impression. I loathed the idea of having an intimate talk to remind him I was with James and was happy, but how awkward would that be if those weren't his intentions?

I forced a smile. "Sure, my mind was wandering."

"How's James?"

My smile deliberately widened. "Great. We're great. Both of us are looking forward to getting out of town for a few days."

CHASING ME

He nodded thoughtfully. "Key West, right? Sounds fun." Brian paused. "Did he tell you we ran into each other earlier in the week?"

I frowned. "What do you mean?"

Brian shrugged. "He came looking for you, and we chatted a bit in my office."

Jessica overheard our conversation and cut in. "James is one hunk of a specimen," she said teasingly, giving me a naughty wink. "Quinn definitely scored in that department."

My cheeks heated, but I knew Jessica enjoyed a good banter. "Hands off, girlfriend."

Jessica grinned and put her hands up. "Fine, fine. Brian, you're gonna have to hook me up with one of your friends, dude. Someone who looks like James. Golden hair, blue eyes, slamming body. I'll close my eyes and pretend." She batted her lashes, and I laughed.

"I gotta go. See you guys later." Brian slid out of the booth, ignoring everyone's protests, peeled off some cash, and left it on the table. "You got one more round, then I want you guys home."

He left without turning back, and once again, I felt as if I was missing a huge piece of the puzzle. Why hadn't James told me about their conversation? I knew James got jealous easy, but it was weird how he didn't even mention the exchange.

Maybe I'd try to talk to him tonight and find out what was going on. I glanced at my watch, then pulled out my phone. I hadn't heard the text come in.

Babe, gonna be at the studio late. Breakfast in bed tomorrow?

I tapped out my response. *Pancakes and bacon?*

A few seconds later, a smiley face popped up. *Definitely. Love you.*

Love you, too.

I finished my Coke, pondering our relationship. We'd come so far since we met in Key West. From a week of sun, sand, and sex, into the bustling city of Chicago, we'd both grown up and grown even closer. I loved how he was strong enough to say "Fuck you" to his parent's money and try things on his own. I'd only fallen deeper in love with him this past year, knowing in an odd way, we'd been waiting for the other in order to feel whole.

Suddenly, I just needed to see him. Maybe I'd surprise him at the studio. It had been a long time since I was able to drop by and see his work. There was something so intimate about watching him sketch, and I craved to be in his presence. We'd also have a safe place to talk. James liked to bury himself in his art when he was working out issues. Maybe it was the best place to really dig deep.

I grabbed my jacket and purse, said goodbye to my friends, and headed out.

Chapter Fifteen
James

I HAD NO CLUE THE DAY would turn into the biggest clusterfuck of my life.

I should've known by the crappy start. After being with Quinn, I felt as if I could handle anything thrown my way, so I started out strong. I'd already accepted I didn't get into the expo, but then had to deal with a crappy shift at Joe's, where I spilled an expensive cup of mocha from burning my damn hand, and was stalked by a bunch of giggly teens who lingered far too long at the tables, watching me.

Ugh.

I spent the rest of the day researching other art schools and hitting the pavement at various stores and museums, asking for applications while well-dressed receptionists wrinkled their noses at me, asking me first what my degree was in.

I didn't care. In fact, I began sifting through the idea of doing something completely different. I'd take extra shifts at Joe's, maybe add another odd job for the money, and build my own collection. Then I'd use the Internet to market it. I'd noticed some craft stores where artists gave up a percentage of commission to sell. Hell, I'd take the time to build my contacts, and create my own shit. I didn't need Ava or the Brush Institute to validate my talent, and if I tapped into my own drive, I'd build something on my own.

I headed to the studio, feeling stronger about my direction, and when I got there a big crowd had formed around a posted piece of paper in the hallway.

"What's going on?" I asked a pretty blonde, who was leaning against one of the art cases.

"The artists for the expo were picked."

"Oh." I didn't even bother, not wanting to depress myself any further. I headed toward my workroom to set up for class, already prepping for my confrontation with Ava. I wouldn't let her win. She'd probably made all that shit up just to cover her ass for not picking me for the expo. I was over it.

I was laying out my charcoal pencils when Tony, a guy from my class, came rushing in. "Dude! Did you see? I can't believe it."

"See what?"

He stood there, gaping. "The expo, man. Your name is listed. You made it!"

I blinked. Wondered if I'd heard right. Then, shaking my head, I raced back down the hallway and pushed my way into the crowd so I could read the list.

#4 – James Hunt.

What the fuck? I stood in shock while the students clapped me on the shoulder, offering their congratulations. Impossible. She'd picked me even after our episode.

But why?

I should have been over the fucking moon, but my gut clenched with worry. Something was off. I needed to talk to her, make sure she wasn't playing any mind games with me. My head spun, but already, the possibility had been extended, and now I wanted it so badly I couldn't think of having it yanked away from me. Would she blackmail me?

No, she should have known I'd never agree to do anything that would hurt my relationship with Quinn, even for the expo. I tried to calm my beating heart, act cool, and wait for Ava to show up and make some sense of it.

She never did.

Instead, another instructor came into class, explaining he'd be taking over for the day. He congratulated the students who'd made the list, and everyone clapped for me since I was the only one from Ava's class to get in.

Shit. I wouldn't get my answers yet.

My head wasn't in the right place, but I tried to make the best of it, using the class time to try to clear my mind by losing myself in work.

I checked my watch and decided to get something to eat. I kept thinking of Brian's words, warning me I'd never be good for Quinn. I turned over Ava's declaration that Quinn wasn't a good fit. It seemed no matter who I spoke with, everyone was against us. Normally, it would make me want to fight harder, but the doubt had been seeded, and I was afraid it was starting to sprout.

Would she be better off without me? Was I being a selfish prick by not letting her go?

I didn't know how long I'd brooded and thought and pondered. It seemed like no matter how hard I fought or tried to get into positive space, my doubts roared over me like a monster hiding under the bed.

I finally decided to do the only thing that made sense. Work. I quickly texted Quinn I'd be at the studio till late and offered her breakfast in bed, then headed back. Maybe if I immersed myself into the only world that ever made sense, I'd find the answer to this world. Scoffing at my philosophical thoughts, I decided to go for oils, setting up a brilliant white canvas before me. I stared at the blank space, relishing that first moment of competition, the stare-down between artist and canvas, the challenge on who would win. My blood warmed and my head cleared, and I attacked, letting all the mess flow through my brush and out.

I worked like a demon, losing myself, without any idea how much time had passed. Eventually, I began to surface, splatters of paint on my shirt, my hand cramped, and I blinked, coming to.

"Not bad."

I jumped, whirling around. Ava stood behind me, studying the swirl of bold colors and jagged lines that made out a couple kissing, wrapped up in each other, pressed against the wall. I'd used colors rather than blacks and whites, and sketchy, rough figures rather than fleshed-out people, giving it an almost crazy, Picasso-like image I'd never experimented with before. It was weird, but arresting, forcing you to try to figure things out. I wasn't even sure what I was trying to say with the piece, but it didn't matter.

Anger shot through me, but I was still a bit weak from the burst of creative work. "What are you doing here?"

"Needed to catch up on some work. See, this is more structured with the lines here." She brushed her finger over air, following the curves of the woman's body and hidden face. "Yet you got messy and real. You're fucked-up in the head right now, huh?"

I stared at this demon creature who somehow managed to beat me up in the same statement she gave me a compliment. I studied her for a while, trying to figure her out. She wore another of her favorite black pantsuits, but it was tight, hugging every part of her body, and the red tank underneath her jacket showed an impressive amount of cleavage. Her hair was scraped back from her face again. I couldn't decide if she was wildly attractive or just plain scary, with the slight sneer on her too-full bloodred lips, white skin, and sharp features.

"Are you proud of yourself?" I asked. "You're the one who fucked up my head. Why did you put me in the show?"

She laughed, shaking her head slowly. "Isn't that what you wanted? What you've been fighting for since day one? If you don't want the slot, let me know now, and I'll give it to another student."

I seethed with frustration, aching to shake her until she dealt with me on a straight level. "Of course I want it! You said in your office I wouldn't get it."

She arched a brow. "No, I never said that. I wanted to find out if you'd be committed and figure out your true intentions. Now, I know. I'm taking a chance on you, Mr. Hunt. But you better make sure you show me this." She jerked a thumb toward my painting. "And not some of that boring crap you tried to pass off as real art. Enjoy your night."

She walked away without a backward glance.

The stress of the past weeks finally broke. My confusion and worry over Quinn. The doubts about myself. And the way my safe place—my art—had suddenly turned into a mind-game explosion due to one raging bitch who wanted to screw with me.

Tendrils of rage licked at my nerve endings, driving me forward. I threw down my brush and followed her into the office, my fists clenched. She looked up from a pile of papers as if I was a minor annoyance. "Yes?"

"I've had enough," I ground out. "How am I expected to work with you? Let you mentor me when I don't trust you? When I know you're just waiting to tie me up in knots because you think I work better when I'm miserable?"

Ava rose from her chair in one graceful motion. Locking my gaze on hers, she strode toward me with slow, deliberate paces. "I'll use anything at my disposal if it makes you better," she drawled. "But let's be honest. You didn't come into this office to talk, did you?"

Shock left me speechless. Not even realizing what I was doing, I backed up until I hit the wall, staring at her in growing discomfort. Holy hell, she thought I wanted to sleep with her. Was I giving off that impression? Sure, she reeked of sex and drama. Back in the day, I would've devoured her whole, not giving a shit because I had a feeling Ava was the mistress of all sex and mind games. We would've happily torn each other apart until we finally parted, exhausted and shattered into tiny pieces.

In that one moment, I had a decision to make. I could choose Quinn and fight for what we had. Or I could slip back into my old shit. Ava would push me further and harder than I ever could imagine. She'd probably make me a star. I'd never have to hide the raw, primitive side of me I tried so desperately to keep in check for Quinn, sweet, sexy, giving Quinn. My brain clicked furiously, trying to choose, while she moved closer until she paused before me, her husky laugh raking across my ears.

I gathered the last of my rage and frustration and battled for the woman I loved. "Fuck you."

Her eyes filled with the challenge, and I knew she relished my fight. I was only a pawn to her in a lifelong game I no longer wanted to play.

"Why don't you fuck me instead?"

I should've pushed her away, because I knew right then, I'd choose Quinn every time.

But I didn't.

Her mouth pressed against mine, and those few seconds in my world were to be the ones that destroyed me. I registered her scent, the tip of her tongue ready to plunge, the way her tits pressed up against my chest. But my body cried for Quinn, my mind locking into place, and I was about to shake her off when a low, guttural cry broke through the air.

Ava turned. My gaze lifted.

Shocked brown eyes stared into mine.

Quinn.

"Quinn!" My lips formed her name, horror washing over me in waves as I realized what she saw and believed. My horror increased when I realized that in those few seconds I'd hesitated, I lost the only choice that kept me alive.

My love for Quinn.

I shoved Ava away and went after Quinn.

CHASING ME

"Don't—j-just don't!" She turned, and I quickly closed the distance, reaching out to grab her arm. "Leave me alone!" she screamed. I stopped in my tracks, and then she was sobbing and running away from me, and I watched my life shatter into pieces around me.

Chapter Sixteen
Quinn

I KNEW HE'D COME AFTER ME. I also knew he'd break down the door, and even though I hated him, I had to hear his story. Why he'd betrayed me. What I'd done wrong to place my trust in him when he'd been lying the whole time.

I didn't know how much time had passed. I sobbed and rocked myself, and then finally, the anger hit, so deep and hard, it shook my body like a storm, and I could barely hang on.

He knocked on the door. "Quinn? Please open up. Please."

He had his key, but allowed me the dignity of decision. I swiped at my swollen eyes, got up from the floor, and flung open the door.

Oh, he reeked of guilt. From his distressed, grief-stricken expression to the dim light in his eyes. I almost lost it again, but I was too mad. "How long have you been fucking her?" I finally asked, feeling the bitter words hurt my tongue.

"I'm not. I never was. I'm here to tell you everything."

"How kind of you." I watched him walk in, shut the door, then shove his hands in his jeans pockets. Those burnished waves I'd slid my fingers through tumbled over his brow. His jacket couldn't hide the bulk of his muscles or the lean thighs encased in worn, faded jeans I loved to pull off him as he tumbled me onto the bed. Raw pain sizzled through me, making me want to double over in agony, but I held my position and glared at him with all the loathing I had. "I thought you hated her. I had no idea that was how you hated someone."

He dragged in a breath and met my gaze. Those sky-blue eyes held an array of pain and guilt, but remained drilled on mine, refusing to look away. "Yes. I need to tell you the story from the beginning, Quinn. Everything I said was true. She ripped me apart in class, disparaged my work, and I never thought I'd get into the expo. One day, she asked to see me after class. I walked into her office and found her blowing the nude model we had in class. It was so fucked-up. I was pissed at her, and I didn't know what she was doing."

"And you didn't go to administration?" I challenged.

He shook his head. "No. I didn't know what to tell them at first. I was afraid they'd think I was making shit up to get into the expo. I finally confronted her, and she gave me this bullshit excuse about needing to push me in order for me to be a better artist."

The ridiculous explanation made no sense. "What are you talking about?" I asked, my voice going higher. I wrapped my arms around my body in an attempt to keep my sanity. "Giving another guy a blow job helps strengthen your art?"

He dragged a hand through his hair. "No. Well, kind of. She said when she pushed me to get in touch with my darker emotions, it was reflected in my work. She said if she picked me for the expo, she'd make sure I succeeded, but I had to push my limits. Said my relationship with you was making me play it safe, and I wasn't built for calm, committed relationships."

My head spun. I began pacing, trying to make sense of all the bullshit being spouted at me by the man I loved. "I'm having a hard time understanding this. She was coming on to you, wasn't she? Saying I was holding you back, and giving you ridiculous excuses so you'd sleep with her. And you bought it, hook, line, and sinker. Why didn't you tell me any of this? Did you want to sleep with her the whole time?"

"No! I never wanted to sleep with her, Quinn, I swear to God. I got confused, and was trying to figure out her game. I'd decided to go to administration the day you told me you got the job, but I didn't want to ruin your good news, and then a few days later, my name was on the list and I found out I got into the expo."

"Because she wants you, James! She's using the expo to blackmail you, or warp your mind about your art. And you chose to accept it all!"

His jaw clenched. "I was trying to understand. Sort things out. Fuck, Quinn, how do you think it makes me feel to be a liability to you? A fucking noose around your neck? Even Brian saw it, and he warned me away from you."

My mouth fell open. Now he was using Brian as an excuse? "What are you talking about? Why didn't you ever tell me you spoke to Brian?"

"I came to see you the night you got the news about the job. Brian called me into his office, and basically told me you were going places, but I'd bring you down. Said you deserved someone who wouldn't break your heart."

I wanted to throw accusations at him, prove he was lying, but I knew he told the truth. Brian did have other intentions toward me, but instead of being direct, he went through James. Disappointment cut deep. Would I still be able to work with him, knowing he'd tried to break us up? I shook off the thought. I had to concentrate on James right now.

"Is that why you slept with her?" I asked bitterly. "Because you figured you'd fail me anyway, so why not grab a few orgasms with your hot teacher?"

"No! Damnit, Quinn, I love you so fucking much you'll never realize. I texted you I was working late, and Ava came in, and I finally confronted her. Asked why she put me into the expo. We had words, and all of a sudden, she's on me, and I was about to push her away when you walked in."

I choked on my temper. "She was kissing you, James! Her mouth on yours! I bet there was plenty of time to stop her, or not let her get near you, but you didn't. I saw it!"

He took a step forward, his hands out in a plea. "Quinn, the truth is, for one moment I wondered if I should let you go. I'm so tired of feeling like I'm gonna fuck up your life. Look at you! You're graduating, with a full-time job, and you're on the road to a successful life. I can't even get through art school, and I'm a trust-fund baby with no skills. Your father hates me. My parents called and let me know I'm an embarrassment to the family because I'm serving fucking coffee to my millionaire friends. I feel like I'm always chasing myself. I'm a loser!"

"You are not a loser!" I screamed at him. "You're the man I loved, but you did the same thing you did in Key West when you accused me of cheating. You took the easy way, letting yourself believe you weren't worthy of me, like I'm some kind of fucking saint! I thought you changed. I thought you believed in us."

My voice broke, along with my heart, and I watched him lose it. He threw back his head and yelled a bunch of curse words, as if he realized we were dying right in front of him and there was nothing left to do. My eyes filled with tears, and I was breaking in two, looking at the man who held my heart and had stomped on it because he'd given up.

"I didn't kiss her back."

Red hazed my vision. I was reminded of all those weak excuses men used when caught cheating. *She didn't mean anything. I was drunk. I never had sex with that woman.* "You didn't push her away!" I choked out. "She was right there, pressed against your dick, her lips near yours. Why didn't you push her away?"

"I froze, Quinn! I kept thinking I was going crazy. She was my teacher, and the key to getting into the expo, which I wanted so fucking bad I didn't realize what she was doing. When she came over to me, I went into shock!"

We breathed hard, falling silent. The air pulsed with emotional energy. "I'm sorry," he said brokenly. "I don't want her, and never wanted her. It's only been you. I should've told you all the shit going on, but I was trying to handle it and then it became a clusterfuck."

"Would you have told me about the kiss?"

My question shot at him like a bullet. He jerked, and his brow lifted while his lips pursed an inch. "Yes."

"Lie. You wouldn't have told me."

"What about Brian? Did you keep anything from me about him?"

Had I? Was I just as guilty, trying to figure out who I was and if James fit into my life? I thought over my reactions and dialogue, and realized maybe I was a bit guilty, too. "I sensed he wanted more than a business relationship between us," I finally said. "He never made a move toward me. And if he had, yes, I would have told you. Everything."

"Did you ever think about you and him together? What it would be like?"

I moaned softly, because I had, for a brief time. "Yes. But it wasn't possible. I could never love anyone the way I do you."

My admission should have made things better, but it didn't. The lies and subtle non-truths between us shimmered like an unscalable wall.

The fight died in me, and all that was left was ashes. The ashes of us.

"We can work this out," he said. He took a few steps toward me, but I couldn't bear to get close, not like this. Not when we were so broken. "We love each other. I'll quit the Brush Institute. Find another way. Hell, I'll go to administration in the morning and tell them everything. Pull out of the expo. Work harder on myself. We can do this."

I didn't say anything. My head hurt and my heart ached, and I just wanted to crawl into bed and sleep so I didn't have to think anymore.

"I need time," I whispered. "I can't do this now."

"Okay." He swiped at his eyes, which looked damp, and nodded. "I understand. I just need you to believe me."

I kept my silence.

"I love you, Quinn."

He turned and left me alone.

Chapter Seventeen

James

TWO DAYS.

She'd left me alone for two days, refusing to answer my texts or calls. I knew Quinn would come back to me when she was ready, but the sick pit in my stomach burned acid up my throat and didn't allow me to do anything but stay at my place. Brooding. Drinking.

Waiting.

I went over the scene a thousand times in my head, cursing myself for not shoving Ava away the moment she came near me, instead of just standing there like an asshole. Quinn was right. I'd had my chance, and blew it because all my doubts made me wonder briefly if I should just fuck Ava and free Quinn for good. The knowledge kept me up all night, filled with guilt and a dark fear she'd end up leaving me for good.

But that wouldn't happen. Quinn and I loved each other too much to let go without a fight.

As the thought tumbled through my head, a knock sounded at the door.

I lurched over and flung it open. She stood before me, dressed in jeans, a purple sweater, and boots. Her dark, silky hair spilled over her shoulders in pin-straight strands I adored running my fingers through. Her dark eyes stared back at me, wide and serious, with something gleaming in the depths I didn't want to face. I knew I'd do anything to keep her.

Anything.

She didn't speak, just walked in and shut the door behind her. I knew I looked like a wreck in sweats, an old T-shirt, and bare feet. Thank God I'd brushed my teeth.

"I missed you," I finally said.

She blinked, her voice soft. "I missed you, too."

"I've thought about what happened between us, Quinn. Over and over. I know I fucked up in a lot of ways, but I think we'll be stronger moving forward now."

She swallowed, her gaze dropping a few inches. My heart beat so loud I couldn't seem to hear anything else. "I don't know if I can forgive you."

I jerked back. Pain slammed through me like I'd just gone a few rounds in the ring. *No. No, no, no...* "You need more time," I forced out. "You need to realize I didn't know what I was doing. I'm pulling out of the expo, Quinn. I'm done. I'm withdrawing from the school, and I'll move forward and do this on my own."

"I don't want you to," she said. "I think you need to deal with Ava on your own and make some decisions, but you should not pull out of the show. You worked too hard, you're too talented, and you deserve it. Don't let her take that from you, James!"

"I don't want anything if I don't have you."

She choked through her next words. "I'm going to Key West. Alone. I want to be with my friends and have some time to myself. I don't know if I can be with you anymore."

I knew I should have been patient and understanding. I should have been the grown-up man I always craved to be, but that dark, raw hunger and need for her rose up from my gut and took over. I grasped her shoulders and pulled her close, my hands tangling in her hair, forcing her head to tilt back. Immediately, I watched her pupils dilate; her lips parted, and I knew she wanted me even then, even when she was disgusted and angry and full of pain. We had a connection that ran deeper than we ever understood, and I shook with the need to show her how good we were together.

"Don't say that," I ground out. I leaned in so my mouth was inches from hers. "Do you think I'm just going to let you walk out of my life without a fight? I'll do anything necessary to keep you, Quinn. Anything."

Her eyes lit up with a furious need that mirrored my own. I watched as the spark ignited, knew when the sexual hunger began to burn out of control, mocking anything else but the craving to be naked with each other, entwined, connected in the only way that ever made sense. Her voice trembled. "You think sex can solve this?" she threw out. Her body shook. "I don't think so. In fact, now I know the reason you've held back with me. You were saving it for your fucking teacher."

I stared at her in pure shock. "What are you talking about?"

"You used to rip me apart with your need to get inside me. But now you're controlled. Oh, you're a great lover, and can wring a string of orgasms from me, but there's something missing. Now I know what it is."

Holy shit. She thought my desperate need to control my inner animal was an insult? A sign I wanted someone else? The past few months of how hard I tried to give her what I thought she expected flashed before me, and I finally realized how wrong I'd been. Quinn could take anything I gave her. She probably reveled in the primitive way I claimed her. Of course she'd wondered why I suddenly changed. I groaned in frustration. I tried to explain. "Quinn, I was trying to change for you! It had nothing to do with Ava, or any other woman. You're the one I want with my last dying breath. I didn't want to treat you like an animal! I wanted to give you romance, and passion, and sweetness. I wanted to adore every part of you in the way you deserve."

"Whatever you want to tell yourself," she tossed out. "I'm done with this conversation."

In a flash, I realized the only thing to do was unveil my real self again. The man I truly was, dark, and dirty, and possessive. Raw and uncivilized. For her. Only her.

My grip tightened. "You're not going anywhere," I growled. "You think I'm going to let you fly off to Key West without proving what you mean to me? I'm done with the lies, and pretending to be someone else with you. Someone I believed you deserved."

"I never wanted you to pretend!" she shouted.

"Good," I growled, yanking her head back. I lowered myself over her. "Because I'm going to fuck you so long and hard you'll never forget it again."

"Fuck you!"

My mouth slammed down on hers, and I was lost.

Her taste always drugged me, but knowing I could lose her drove me into insanity. I held her as my tongue thrust past her lips, conquering her sweet, wet mouth while I backed her up until she slammed against the wall.

She fought me for a while, twisting and trying to get away, but I also knew how bad she wanted me to conquer her, how she craved to feel that wild high when I fucked her, so I kept my grip firm and my kiss deep, until she began to soften, trembling beneath me, and then I had her. But I also needed the words.

"Tell me you want this, Quinn." I bit her lip, and she moaned. "Tell me, or I'll stop."

She shuddered. "I want this."

This wasn't about finesse or gentleness. This was about a primitive claiming of man to his mate. I kissed her hard, bruising her lips, soothing with my tongue, and yanked her sweater and bra off. Keeping my knee pressed against between her thighs to hold her in place, I ducked my head and sucked on her nipple. She cried out, arching up for more, and I bit and licked and plumped her tits, drowning in her gorgeous, clean scent, reveling in the smooth silkiness of her pale skin. My mouth never paused as my fingers deftly unsnapped her jeans and pushed them, along with her underwear, to her ankles. She was still wearing her boots.

Quinn wiggled to kick the fabric loose, but I stilled her, dropping to my knees as I licked her navel, pressing my lips to her mound, breathing in her musky arousal, knowing she'd drip over my fingers with her excitement.

"I love your sweet pussy," I murmured. "Love how you clench around my cock when I push inside you. Love the way you cream for me and draw blood on my back when you get too excited. You're so fucking beautiful."

She panted in response to my dirty talk, and I was disgusted with myself for denying both of us the excitement of being everything we wanted in the bedroom. When had I decided to be a nice guy when I made love to my woman? When had I lost my way?

"I want you to come against my tongue," I ordered.

"Oh, God, James, don't—"

"Come hard, Quinn." I pushed her pink lips apart and attacked her pussy, licking at her hard clit with sharp, stinging strokes that pumped her to the edge fast, my fingers curling and plunging into her wet channel, that hot, sweet cunt sucking me in deep and begging for more. She screamed and writhed against my mouth, and I went wild, parting her wider, using the flat of my tongue over her dripping slit, then circling her throbbing clit until I finally closed my teeth around the nub and bit gently.

She came hard, thrashing her head against the door, and I swallowed every drop, making sure to extend her climax. I yanked off her boots, pulling off her pants and underwear, then stood up. Her hands grabbed at me, halfway drunk with pleasure, but I held her off, shoving down my pants in one quick movement and grabbing her knee. Bending slightly, I hooked my knee under her left thigh and dragged open her legs.

"Wrap your arms around my neck."

She did, shaking, and I growled my approval and bit her neck. She shuddered and cried out again. "Hold on tight, Quinn. My cock needs to be inside you, needs to be swallowed whole by your gorgeous cunt, which is all pink and wet and glistening." I pushed myself inside until I was buried deep. My eyes rolled to the back of my head, it felt so fucking good, so tight and hot, squeezing my dick mercilessly.

"James!"

"That's right, baby, scream my name, I'm the only one who can make you come like this, aren't I? Now, give it to me, all of it." Hoisting her up against the door, I lifted her high and slammed her back down on my cock. She cried out, and I did it again, lifting and thrusting, over and over, going so deep inside her I didn't know where I ended and she began. I took her like the animal I was, rough and raw, with no finesse or anything tender, and she loved every fucking second of it. Her nails dragged down my back, my mouth bit her neck, and she was coming and screaming against me, and I never stilled my thrusting until I exploded and splashed my semen inside her, marking her for good, marking her as mine.

Sweaty, exhausted, we sank to the floor in a tangle of naked limbs and clothes surrounding us. I smoothed back her hair, and we tried to catch our breath. Peace settled over me, and a rightness reminding me Quinn was the other half of my soul. I'd never question myself, or us together, again.

"I never meant to make you doubt how much I want you," I said. "I was stupid. Trying to be a man I thought was better for you."

She blinked, her face still sad. "I want so much for us," she said slowly. "But the most important is just to be ourselves and love each other. No lies."

"No lies."

I smiled and pressed a kiss to her forehead. "Let me make you some dinner."

"No, James. I have to leave. Nothing's changed."

I stared at her like an idiot. What? Hadn't we just made up? "Quinn, what are you talking about? I thought I made you understand."

She rolled to her feet and put on her clothes. "You did. But there's still too many doubts. All I can think of is you kissing that woman. It's burned in my memory."

"I explained that—"

"I know! I know what you explained, and I know my body weeps for yours! I know I love you more than anyone, and I don't want to live without you! But I still need some time and distance. Sex won't fix it. I'm going to Key West without you. I'm sorry."

I thought of her, free in Key West, surrounded by her friends, surrounded by temptation. She didn't need me after all. She was strong enough to leave me behind and make it on her own. My gut twisted, and I watched her walk to the door, her chin tilted upward in that move of determination I knew so well.

"I love you, James. I just need to figure out if it's enough for us."

She left.

Chapter Eighteen
Quinn

SOMETHING HAD ALMOST broken when I left him last night.

I wanted to stay. Wanted to weep and take him back in my arms and forgive him. I knew he didn't love or want Ava. Knew it was a stupid mistake he regretted. But there was so much more working beneath the surface, I began to wonder if I was good for him.

He'd tried to change the core of who he was, in bed and out, to please me. He put me a on a pedestal I never asked for, thinking I was some kind of holy do-gooder meant for gentle hands and sheer adoration. I never wanted that. In Key West, we were equals. We loved each other with an open passion that had no limits, and we never questioned it.

But Chicago had changed so many things. The everyday struggle at life made our island romance feel like a dream. I knew it was real, the way we felt about each other, but I still doubted our future. I needed some time to regroup, think, and make a decision.

But first, I was going to have a chat with Brian.

I headed to New Beginnings and asked Sharon for an appointment. I only had to wait twenty minutes before I stepped into his office.

"Quinn, I thought you were off this week. Big Spring Break."

I studied his face for a while. Kind eyes, thick ginger hair, laugh lines bracketing his full mouth. His crisp button-down shirt and khakis cut a figure of competence. Brian was an amazing man. Besides his drive to make the world better, I sensed he had a good soul. Attractive. Mature. Intelligent. I imagined our life together, matching perfectly in all ways except the only way that truly mattered.

That unknown element that connected two people. I could spend the rest of my life trying to explain it or put it into words, but it was a gut feeling, a sense of rightness in a crazy world. Brian and I didn't have it. Would never have it. The only way I could take the job was if he understood it.

"I leave tonight. But I wanted to talk to you about something."

"Of course. Have a seat." We sat and faced each other. "Is everything okay?"

"I know about your conversation with James."

He stiffened, but nodded, not denying it. "Okay. Well, I told him some things I'm sure he shared. Are you here because you're upset with me?"

I sighed. "I'm here because I need to tell you the truth. I thought about us, Brian. I imagined what we would be like if I chose you over James. But I can also tell you it will never happen. I admire you and like you as a friend. I respect you as a boss and the director of the clinic. If James and I broke up, I still wouldn't date you. We're not meant to be, but I don't feel comfortable taking this job if you don't truly understand. We'll be working long hours together, and if you can't get past it, I need to decline the position."

Relief cut through me. There. It was out, and though I hated the idea of losing the job I'd worked so hard for, I couldn't deal with the tension between us or the constant concern from James if we did stay together.

Brian looked startled and leaned over the desk. "I'm sorry, Quinn. Sorry I put you in this position or gave you the wrong idea. I do like you, and I see things in you and James that remind me of my ex-wife. But I stepped over the line, especially telling your boyfriend he's not good enough for you. What do I know? There is no one that could fill the position like you. And I promise, there will be no tension or questionable moves on my part. Do you believe me?"

I looked into his brown eyes and saw the truth. He may have been attracted to me, but he'd never let that take priority over the clinic. I saw the honesty in his face and the apology in his gaze.

I smiled. "I believe you. Thanks, Brian."

"You're welcome. I'm glad you came to me. Have a good time on vacation. Come back rested and ready to work."

I laughed and rose from my chair. "I will."

I went home and packed, my soul lighter and feeling as if one door had closed, leaving another open. I still didn't know what I was going to do about James, but all I wanted was to hug my girlfriends, have a Sex on the Beach, and talk it out.

Chapter Nineteen
James

I'D LOST HER.

How long had I stayed in my apartment, waiting for some miracle? Waiting for her to come back to me, declare her love, and tell me she wanted to start over?

I realized again I'd made her my world, and then destroyed her. I had no friends, no family, and no career. Sinking into the depths of depression, I heard Brian's words in my head, over and over.

You're going to break her heart.

And I had. But as the clock ticked, I came to another surprising truth, and an odd strength began to unfurl deep in my gut.

Quinn loved me, but I needed to get my shit together.

Quinn thought I was deserving and talented, so I needed to believe in myself, too.

I thought over my choices. About how much I loved art, and how Ava had screwed me up, and what I could do about it. About my wrong choices, and how I needed to make a stand to show Quinn I was the man she needed me to be. Yeah, it was gonna be messy, but at least I'd be telling the truth and trying to move forward.

It really wasn't about Brian at all. Or even Ava. It was about my own insecurities, and confusion, and crap. It was about believing and trusting in Quinn and her love for me.

Time to deal with it.

I made the call. Got a meeting with the Dean for 2:00 p.m. I gathered up all my work since the year had started then headed into The Brush Institute.

First, I'd take care of business.

Then I'd go after her.

Chapter Twenty
Quinn

"I CAN'T BELIEVE FIVE days have gone by already," Mac sighed, her familiar wide-brimmed hat hiding her from the sun.

"It's been a hell of a week," Cassie sighed, sipping her own fruit concoction. We had all carved out a few hours to sip cocktails in the sun and enjoy the last of our freedom before our final night.

How different this trip was from last year. Yes, we still sipped our Sex on the Beach drinks, and lay in the sun, and teased and laughed with each other. Yes, Mac was still a huge country star hidden behind a stylish hat, and Cassie was still serious and involved in another dangerous case since she'd testified a week ago at trial.

But James wasn't here. It had nothing to do with the yacht, or his mansion, or the wild parties. I missed him so bad, my body wept with the pain. His smile, his touch, his laugh. I missed the way he used to put his hand at the small of my back when we walked together, in protection and possession. I missed the way he knew I hated beer, and liked things tidy, and needed to help others in order to feel whole. I loved the way he held me in his arms, with all the rough passion I needed to be completely alive. I loved who I was when I was with him.

Mac peered at me from under the shadowed brim. "You miss him."

I laughed. They knew me best. When I'd first arrived and told them everything, they'd cursed James and vowed to kill him. It was only later, when I discussed how the last six months had developed between us, telling them about Brian and what Ava had done, that they began to understand, and grudgingly told me if I forgave James, they would, too.

"Yeah."

Cassie gave me a searching look. "You're ready to forgive him, aren't you?"

Slowly, I nodded. I had needed the time away to see what life was like without James. And I realized something else. I could live without him. I was strong, capable, and would find love again.

But I didn't want to.

I wanted to forgive, rebuild, and go on stronger than before. Wasn't that what real love was about? Messiness and mistakes and some pain in order to appreciate the good stuff? Deciding what I could and couldn't live with? I'd learned so much about myself and James this past year. I wasn't ready to let it go.

"Good," Mac announced. "I hate seeing you unhappy. And it seems like James is your true fit. Your other half."

I smiled and reached out, linking my hands with theirs. "I love you guys. I haven't seen you as much this past year," I said. "Can we make a vow to do this every Spring Break? Whether we bring boys or not?"

My girls nodded and raised their glasses. "Absolutely. To us. Best friends."

We all clinked glasses and smiled. "But the party isn't over yet," Mac reminded us. "Captain Crowe's tonight for a surprise."

"No hint?" I asked teasingly.

"Nope. We'll all meet there."

"Are you going to call James and tell him?" Cassie asked.

I shook my head. "We need to talk in person. When I get back to Chicago, hopefully, he'll be ready to move forward. Or not."

"He will," Mac said forcefully. "He's nuts about you. Even if he is broke now."

Cassie and I laughed. "But more honorable," Cassie added. "And much more of a man deserving of Quinn. Better than the rich dude with the asshole friends."

We all drank and then went our different ways for the rest of the afternoon.

I dressed a bit more carefully for the last night. Black skirt, strappy sandals—flats, not heels, since I still sucked walking in them—and a silvery tank that shimmered when I walked. Something fun and flirty to make myself feel good. I headed down Duval Street, enjoying the mad revelry of the crowds, drinking and shouting, laughing and dancing in honor of the sunset. I strolled slowly, the sun burning my shoulders, remembering how James used to keep slathering suntan lotion on me because of my fair skin, and suddenly, tears stung my eyes. All I wanted was to call him and tell him I loved him.

I would.

Screw it. I'd tell Mac and Cassie I needed to talk to him, right then and there, and find someplace private and call him and—

A familiar figure was moving toward me. The sun blocked my view and I blinked furiously, wondering why those burnished waves and that tall, lean body looked like James. He walked forward with a determined purpose, gaze narrowed on me, and suddenly the crowds parted and he was in front of me. Those beloved stinging-blue eyes, filled with need and a bit of wariness, stared into mine. My breath caught.

"James?"

I couldn't say anything else. He leaned forward, cupped my cheeks, and bent my head. Kissed me with a purity and tenderness that broke through my soul. Then slowly, he lifted his head.

"I couldn't stay away, Quinn. I love you, and I'll follow you to the ends of the earth. Your heart is part of mine—I'm only half a man without you. Forgive me. Give me another chance."

I broke open and gave him everything I had. "Yes," I breathed against his lips. "I don't want a life without you. I want another chance together, stronger than before. I love you."

He growled and lifted me in his arms, kissing me passionately. He swung me around in the middle of Duval Street, and I knew everything would be okay.

"I was going to call you," I said when he put me down. "I couldn't stand being without you another second."

"And I wanted to give you enough time to yourself, but I knew I'd follow you anywhere. Listen, Quinn, I went to the Brush Institute. I spoke with administration and told them everything about Ava."

I stiffened. It still hurt a bit, but most of the sharpness had faded. "What happened?"

"We had a meeting, and two other students came forward. Both male. They admitted to being pursued by Ava, and there's an investigation being done."

I let out a sigh of relief. No other student should go through that, not when they just wanted to learn a craft. "What about the show?"

"I told them I was pulling out of the show, but Lucas—the other art teacher who mentors students—saw my work. He came to the house and asked me to stay. Said I had enough talent on my own and to stop questioning my abilities. He said he sees huge things for me, Quinn, and he had tons of connections. He wants to take me on."

I squealed and hugged him hard. "I knew it! I knew you'd do it on your own. I'm so proud of you, baby."

He kissed me again and laughed with joy. "Let's celebrate."

"Cassie and Mac are at Captain Crowe's. There's going to be a surprise."

"Well, let's go and say hello to the crew."

We walked hand-in-hand to the bar where we'd hung out last year, and dove into the mad crowd, having fun drinking and chattering, the music loud and full of life. We caught up with Cassie, who hugged both of us when we told her we were back together, and suddenly Mac was climbing to the front of the bar in a surprise concert that pumped up the crowd. She called out a special dedication, and then Austin was beside her, and they were singing and looking at each other with such love, I knew they'd finally found their happily-ever-after ending.

We filled the rest of the hours with drinks and laughter. I noticed Cassie and Ty talking at the bar, and I had a good feeling they might be able to re-connect. They fit so well together.

Later, when darkness had fallen and the moon was full, James and I walked barefoot on the beach where we had shared our first kiss. "You're so fucking beautiful," he said huskily. "I look at you now and love you even more. You're it, Quinn. You're the woman who makes me whole. I want to strip off this little black skirt, lay you in the sand, and fuck you long and hard until the sun comes up."

I lifted on tiptoes, the warm surf swirling around my ankles, and dragged his head down.

"What are you waiting for?" I whispered naughtily.

So he did.

Epilogue
James

SO, MAYBE THIS IS A LOVE STORY.

We flew back from Key West and decided to move in together. Quinn graduated with honors and flung herself into her new job at the clinic, spearheading a new program that almost doubled their clients. I was so fucking proud of her. She was good for this world, her inner light spilling out to everyone she met, a reminder of everything pure and right.

For me? Well, I worked frantically, building new pieces, and the expo was a huge success. Lucas pushed me hard, harder than Ava ever had, in a different way, and I came out with a bunch of offers and contacts. Another year or two, and I may even be able to open up my new studio, but right now, the money is good, and I finally got to quit Joe's. I work odd hours at the studio, and there's some travel involved, but I'm finally living my dream, on my own terms.

And us? We're strong. The problems with Ava helped us rebuild our foundation. I'm not trying to change my way for her anymore, and I finally believe I'm worth something. I'm coming into myself a bit more every day, and she steps back and lets me find my way. Loves me anyway. And when she's in my arms? She gives me everything she's got, no holds barred. She fucks me with the intensity of a woman who has given her body and soul, her mind and heart, and that's all I ever wanted.

I'm going to ask her to marry me soon.

So, yeah. We got lucky. This one is a love story.

I'm so fucking glad I got to write a whole new ending.

More by Jennifer Probst

More Sex on the Beach

BEFORE YOU
By Jenna Bennett

It's all fun and games
I had a simple plan for spring break.
Sun, sand, and a hot guy. Sex on the beach with no strings attached.
A chance to get rid of this pesky virginity once and for all.
And when I met Tyler McKenna, I thought I had it made.

Until someone gets hurt
But then girls started turning up at Key West landmarks. Girls who looked like me, but with one crucial difference: They'd all been drugged and relieved of their virginity.

The virginity I still have. The virginity Ty refuses to take.
And now I've begun to wonder whether there isn't more to him than meets the eye.
Suddenly, sex on the beach doesn't sound so good anymore...

Praise for BEFORE YOU:
"The story felt fun, as Cassie enjoys the sunshine, and things develop and start to sizzle when she meets Ty. It kept me on the edge of my seat...and I was curling my toes at the romance." –*Bella, from A Prairie Girl Reads*

"A thrilling mystery mixed with romance and some much needed humor and wittiness, Before You is an enjoyable and gripping story." –*Stella, Ex Libris*

BETWEEN US
By Jen McLaughlin

I'm just a girl...
I'm a famous country star who's spent her life cultivating a good girl persona to avoid bad press, but I've reached my limit. I'm going away for spring break with my two best friends from college, and we've vowed to spend the vacation seeking out fun in the sun—along with some hot, no-strings-attached sex. The only thing I needed was the perfect guy, and then I met Austin Murphy. He might be totally wrong for me, but the tattooed bad boy is hard to resist. When I'm in his arms, everything just feels *right*.

And I'm just a guy...
I'm just a bartender who lives in Key West, stuck in an endless cycle of boredom. But then Mackenzie Forbes, America's Sweetheart herself, comes up to me and looks at me with those bright green eyes...and everything changes. She acts like she's just a normal girl and I'm just a normal guy, but that couldn't be further from the truth. My past isn't

pretty, you know. I did what I had to do to survive, and she'd run if she learned the truth about my darkness. But with her, I'm finally realizing what it's like to be *alive*. To laugh, live, and be happy.

All good things must come to an end...

Praise for BETWEEN US:
"The sweet good-girl looking to be a bit naughty and the sexy bad-boy looking to be thought of as good…Jen gives us another winning story with BETWEEN US. Drool worthy and devourable with plenty of emotion, I adored this book from start to finish! A must read!" –*Jillian, from Read, Love, Blog*

"Anything that Jen McLaughlin writes is gold, in my book. BETWEEN US is no different. Set in the sweltering heat of Key West, it has all the passion, friendship and drama that made it impossible to put down. Go read this book. You won't be disappointed!" –*Casey, Literary Escapism*

Marriage to A Billionaire Series

"A passion that is explosive as the love that unfolds is tender, a beautiful happily ever after that encompasses everything; Jennifer Probst delivers a fiery and wild romance that goes straight to your heart." ~ Maldivian Book Reviewers – 5 stars

"A charming, fast-paced story full of non-stop sexual tension that crackles off the page. The Marriage Bargain will hook you and leave you begging for more!" ~ Laura Kaye, Author of Hearts in Darkness

"Absolutely amazing! I was hooked from the beginning and couldn't put it down." ~ Kris, Bitten By Paranormal Romance

"THE MARRIAGE BARGAIN is one of the cutest stories I have read in a while. The story is highly amusing and kept me chuckling throughout when I wasn't mopping the tears away." ~ Kay Quintin, Fresh Fiction

"Loved it! 'The Marriage Bargain' had all the ingredients for the making of an amazing story: Childhood friends reunited, Marriage of convenience, Love spell gone astray, opposites attract and great chemistry." ~ Sara, Harlequin Junkie Reviews "I just had to read Jennifer Probst's book after all the buzz about it on Twitter and Amazon and Goodreads, etc, and especially after I'd got an eyeful of that super-sexy cover.... And I can happily say I wasn't disappointed. Yes, what's inside the book is as sexy and gorgeous as that cover." ~ Heidi Rice, USA Today Bestselling Author

THE SEARCHING SERIES

"Witty dialogue and passionate characters . . . a sophisticated, sexy romance with an intelligent, business savvy heroine at its center, and a super-hot love interest."—*RT Book Reviews*

"Bestseller Probst creates a likeable cast [and] refreshing female friendships."—*Publishers Weekly*

"Romance star Probst pens another sexy, satisfying romance"—*Kirkus Reviews*

"Jennifer Probst is one of those feel-good authors. It's always a good romantic comedy. I loved Searching for Perfect…"—5 Stars, *Nestled in a Book*

ABOUT THE AUTHOR

Jennifer Probst is the New York Times, USA Today, and Wall Street Journal bestselling author of both sexy and erotic contemporary romance. She was thrilled her novel, The Marriage Bargain, was the #6 Bestselling Book on Amazon for 2012. Her first children's book, Buffy and the Carrot, was co-written with her 12 year old niece, and her short story, "A Life Worth Living" chronicles the life of a shelter dog. She makes her home in New York with her sons, husband, two rescue dogs, and a house that never seems to be clean. She loves hearing from all readers! Stop by her website at http://www.jenniferprobst.com for all her upcoming releases, news and street team information.

Made in the USA
Middletown, DE
28 May 2016